Michael Underwood and The Murder Room

〉〉〉 This title is part of The Murder Room, our series dedicated to making available out-of-print or hard-to-find titles by classic crime writers.

Crime fiction has always held up a mirror to society. The Victorians were fascinated by sensational murder and the emerging science of detection; now we are obsessed with the forensic detail of violent death. And no other genre has so captivated and enthralled readers.

Vast troves of classic crime writing have for a long time been unavailable to all but the most dedicated frequenters of second-hand bookshops. The advent of digital publishing means that we are now able to bring you the backlists of a huge range of titles by classic and contemporary crime writers, some of which have been out of print for decades.

From the genteel amateur private eyes of the Golden Age and the femmes fatales of pulp fiction, to the morally ambiguous hard-boiled detectives of mid twentieth-century America and their descendants who walk our twenty-first century streets, The Murder Room has it all. 〉〉〉

The Murder Room
Where Criminal Minds Mee

themurderroom.com

Michael Underwood (1916–1992)

Michael Underwood (the pseudonym of John Michael Evelyn) was born in Worthing, Sussex and educated at Christ Church College, Oxford. He was called to the Bar in 1939 and served in the British army during World War Two. He returned to work in the Department of Public Prosecutions until his retirement in 1976, and wrote almost 50 crime novels informed by his career in the law. His five series characters include Sergeant Nick Atwell and lawyer Rosa Epton, of whom is was said by the *Washington Post* that she 'outdoes Perry Mason'.

By Michael Underwood

The Anxious Conspirator

Michael Underwood

An Orion book

Copyright © Isobel Mackenzie 1969

The right of Michael Underwood to be identified as the author of this
work has been asserted in accordance with the Copyright, Designs and
Patents Act 1988.

This edition published by
The Orion Publishing Group Ltd
Orion House
5 Upper St Martin's Lane
London WC2H 9EA

An Hachette UK company
A CIP catalogue record for this book is available from the British Library

ISBN 978 1 4719 0788 3

www.orionbooks.co.uk

To Tim and Suzy

CHAPTER ONE

FREDA FISCHER brushed a strand of hair from her cheek, and with an air of weary patience, put out a hand to retrieve the hefty-looking suitcase which was gliding toward her along the conveyor belt. It was flanked by elegantly matching air travel cases of the sort one sees displayed in shop windows, piled like Chinese boxes. They gave hers the appearance of old tweed at a Dior show of evening wear.

She carried it across to the Customs bench at an awkward trot and inserted herself next to someone who was already receiving attention. With a sigh she puffed the still errant strand of hair out of her eye. Her nose felt shiny and what was left of her lipstick was caking, but she had deliberately refrained from making any running repairs to her face until she was clear of all the formalities of arrival. A glamorous appearance at this moment would not, she had reckoned, be in her best interest.

She had had time, while waiting for the baggage to be disgorged, to study the faces of the Customs officers and it was design which brought her to the particular place where she was now standing. It always struck her that British Customs officers looked as though they rightly belonged on the quarter decks of destroyers. They were so very different from their Continental counterparts who resembled much more the minor Civil Servants which they were, than nautical heroes.

The officer she had selected was young and fresh-complexioned and wore the studiously polite expression which goes with the job. She watched him covertly as he finished with the person on her left and decided she had chosen aright. A second before he arrived in front of her, she cast down her eyes.

'Is this all your baggage, miss?'

'Yes.' She nodded shyly.

'Do you live in this country?'

'No, I am a visitor.'

'Would you read this, please?' She stared at the notice he

1

now held before her like a mirror. 'You understand what it says?'

'Yes.'

'And have you anything to declare?'

'No.' She shook her head slowly as if to emphasise that she regarded the question and her answer as forming a solemn contract between them.

'No cigarettes or liquor: no watches or cameras?'

'No, not any.'

For a few seconds they stared gravely into each other's eyes.

'No gifts of any sort?'

'No.'

'How long will you be staying in this country?'

'Perhaps two weeks I stay.'

She had hoped she wouldn't be asked this particular question, even though it was improbable that the same people would see her again when she left, whether she stayed two days or two months. And anyway she would, as before, make a point of having an excuse ready to explain her premature departure. It would, however, have been unarguable that her suitcase was uncommonly large and heavy for a mere overnight visit.

The Customs officer gave her a small smile.

'Well, have a nice stay,' he said as he made a chalk squiggle on the end of her case and moved away.

She returned his smile shyly and, lifting down the suitcase, prepared to carry it out into the crowded hall past the sea of expectant faces which were clustered round the doorways.

Outside the terminal building, she paused to rest and to sniff the damp misty air of an early March evening. So far, so good. Everything had gone as smoothly as it had last time, and she was once more safely in England.

The Fiat 600 was parked exactly where she had been told to expect it. With the duplicate key she unlocked the driver's door, stowed her suitcase on the back seat and got in herself. Her first act was to set about restoring her face. It was one thing to assume an appealingly waif-like appearance in front of a Customs officer, quite another to do so before the five men who were waiting for her six miles away. By the time she had finished, she again looked the attractive and composed young lady of twenty-four which was her normal air. She gave her face a final examination in the small hand mirror, brushed some invisible specks off the shoulders of her bleached mackintosh and was ready to go.

On reaching the main road, she turned left away from London. In twenty minutes she would be at her destination. A small smile flickered across her face as she recalled the Immigration Officer's concern whether she would be able to support herself financially while in England. She had been able to satisfy him by producing her modest supply of travellers cheques.

Hers, of course, were genuine and quite unlike the £100,000 worth of forged ones which lay concealed in the secret compartment of her very ordinary-looking suitcase.

CHAPTER TWO

IN appearance there were few similarities between the five men who awaited Freda Fischer's arrival in various postures of nervous boredom. One thing which they did share in common, however, was a quality of soft-spokenness to be found among criminals of a certain class. Admittedly George Bromley, their leader, had an ugly rasp to his voice and could shout as loudly as anyone when he chose, but his normal tone was no worse than a hack-saw cutting through bone, and as for the rest of them they always conversed in the quiet, relaxed tones of high financiers, which in a sense they were.

The room in which they were sitting was cheerless and at this moment stiflingly hot. It was the living-room of a wood-built bungalow situated not far from the river midst a haphazard landscape of similar structures.

George Bromley, known as Big George among his fringe acquaintances, sat at the head of the table like a Chairman waiting to call the meeting to order. He was scowling and even a blind canary could have told that he was in an ill-humour.

'She should be here by now,' he said, gazing without affection at each of the others in turn.

'Give her a chance. Her 'plane was due only thirty minutes ago.' Tony Dayne who spoke resembled an amiable rodent.

3

But though he wore a perpetually somnolent and harmless air, he was capable of considerable physical and mental agility when occasion required. He sat, the smallest man in the room, sprawled in the largest chair with one leg dangling idly over the arm.

Bromley ignored him. 'You can never be sure with bloody foreigners. Some of you would do well to remember that.'

'Yes, papa.' Derek Armley said, with a wink at Dayne. He was a young man with a glib manner and a string of predatory girl-friends whose demands virtually ruled out the possibility of an honest life, even if he had so desired.

'Aren't you forgetting who set up this lark, George?' Max Rutter was the oldest man in the room. He had also, under a variety of different names, served more sentences of imprisonment than any of the others. His failing was jewellery: his own. On at least one occasion he had been identified by the two diamond rings he wore on fingers of each hand.

'I thought I asked you not to wear all those rocks on your hands,' Bromley said in a grating voice.

'I don't when I'm out on the job,' Rutter replied. 'But among friends, what's wrong? And anyway you haven't answered my question.'

'What question?'

Rutter smiled tolerantly at the others. 'If you don't trust bloody foreigners, George, why did you take this on in the first place?'

'You know why I did. Because of the money.'

'And it's been O.K. so far, hasn't it? It's been darned good in fact.'

'So far,' Bromley repeated darkly. 'But I still say that you want to watch out when you have dealings with foreigners. You don't think I roped all you lot in until I was satisfied it was a worth-while deal?'

'More worth-while to some than to others,' said Roy Passfield with a sweet smile which served only to underline the taunt.

'What the hell do you mean by that?' Bromley demanded angrily. 'If it's because I do better than you, of course I do. You're paid staff. I'm the manager. If you're not satisfied you can clear out.' A silence followed this exertion of authority and Passfield himself, who had once been a male dancer on television, stared sulkily at his finger-nails.

'Nevertheless,' Bromley went on, thoughtfully studying the faces of his four colleagues, 'I am proposing to have a bit of a showdown when our lady arrives. I don't consider present arrangements are satisfactory and I mean to tell her so.'

'But she's only a courier,' Dayne put in. 'What can she do?'

'She can convey our sentiments to headquarters,' Bromley replied grimly.

'But we don't know anything about headquarters,' said Rutter. 'Or do we? I mean apart from the fact that they're somewhere ... somewhere in Europe.' He glanced quickly at the others.

'It isn't in your interest to know where the stuff's forged.' Bromley pursed his lips. 'Even I don't know the exact location.'

'Or the people we're dealing with, I gather?' Rutter added.

George Bromley never cared having to disclaim omniscience, but realised it was better to do so on this occasion. 'No, I don't know them, either. That's why I intend having things out with the girl when she gets here. She's our only link with the people at the other end.'

'How much is she bringing over?' Dayne asked.

'A hundred thousand.'

Five pairs of eyes became lost in silent contemplation.

'Well, thank God we're operating from London this time,' Passfield said, his expression suddenly brightening. 'Winter in Manchester was almost the death of me. I don't think you others realised what a perishing office that was, but Tony and I were there every day.' He looked across at Tony Dayne for support, but Dayne appeared to be sunk in his own thoughts and only a distant smile flickering across his face indicated that he had been listening at all.

Being more personable than the others, Dayne and Passfield had been given the duties of counter clerks in the office of Snowcap Holidays, with the job of charming clients into signing up for a winter-sports holiday. 'Yes, sir, Snowcap Holidays take care of everything. . . . No, you don't have to worry with your bank, we can supply travellers cheques as well ... so much easier having everything dealt with under one roof.'

5

Later when the rich harvest had been reaped, Snowcap Holidays of Manchester had melted away as completely as the snow to which it had feverishly consigned its gullible clients. And even those people who did happen to notice that the small travel agency on the corner had closed didn't give it a great deal of thought. In an age of mushroom growths, there was nothing particularly remarkable about such an occurrence.

Now, a few weeks later, Suntrap Tours had established themselves in a West London suburb and were ready to open their doors and sell enchanting holidays on Mediterranean beaches.

And after that it would be somewhere in the south-west. Another office, another eye-catching name over the entrance. It all required a fair amount of organisation, but it was sufficiently profitable to enable its operators to contemplate a happy retirement from business before long.

With Dayne and Passfield the front counter boys and Rutter working in a back room as secretary-cum-accountant of the outfit, Bromley and Armley were left free to look after things outside the office and to prepare for the next flit.

In a business of such fat and rapid profits, none had felt the need to know more than he was told. It was sufficient that George Bromley had recruited them six months before and told them that an organisation on the Continent wished to undertake the distribution of forged travellers cheques in England and that this had to be done through a travel agency which would be established for the purpose. The sale of the travellers cheques, which purported to be those of an internationally known banking concern, would provide the retailers with a handsome profit ('it was as good as making the money yourself', Rutter had once observed) and the beauty of the scheme was that, thanks to the domestic ramifications of the bank concerned, it must take at least several months for the forgeries to be spotted—longer still to trace them—by which time the flit was complete.

There was a strict rule, however, that they were not to cash the cheques for their own use, since this would increase the chance of detection. Despite this injunction, the others were aware that Bromley had several times done so, and now he was apparently proposing to send headquarters a message telling them where they got off.

6

'That must be her car now,' Bromley said, breaking the silence which had fallen.

Dayne swung himself out of his chair and crossing to the window peered round the end of the heavy chocolate-coloured curtain.

'It's quite misty out there,' he said with a slight note of worry in his voice. 'Yes, she's just coming up to the door.'

'Go and let her in.' Bromley nodded at Armley, who rose and left the room.

A few seconds later the door opened and Freda entered. She smiled nervously at the faces which were turned in her direction. 'I am sorry if I am late, but it is foggy and I caught a false road.'

'Come in, Freda,' Bromley said affably. 'Is Derek getting your suitcase out of the car?' He smirked at the others while Freda began to unbutton her mackintosh with cold fingers. 'Now you're here,' he went on, 'let's get down to business. You come and sit next to me '

'Yes, it is always gooa to do our business quickly,' Freda rejoined. 'It is not good for me to stay too long.'

At this moment Armley came in carrying the homely-looking suitcase, which he put down between her and Bromley.

'We certainly don't want to keep you,' Bromley said, fixing her with a hard look, 'but there are one or two things to be straightened out.' He paused. 'The lads and I are not too happy about some of the arrangements.'

'I do not make the arrangements,' Freda interrupted in an anxious voice. 'I am only the courier, do you say?'

'But you can convey our sentiments back to headquarters,' Bromley went on. 'There's nothing to prevent your doing that.'

'Why do you not write what you wish to say?'

'Because I think a personal message via you will be more effective. Anyway, I have written and nothing happened.'

Freda looked desperately round the five impassive faces which were turned toward her. 'But I do not know the big bosses of our organisation. I am here only to hand over the cheques and to take back the money for them. . . .'

Bromley scraped a tooth with his thumbnail and appeared to be cogitating. Then he said, 'You see, we don't believe this travel agency lark is the best way of getting rid of the cheques.' It was clear from the expressions on the faces of his companions that they wondered what was coming next. They might or they might not agree. The royal 'we' had, however, alerted them. 'We think there's an easier way without the necessity of all this palaver.'

'But it is laid down by headquarters,' Freda said, urgently. 'It is the best way. Headquarters know. They operate in other countries as well and it is always through a travel agency.'

'I dare say,' Bromley replied, 'but because it happens to be the best way in Italy or France, doesn't mean to say it's the best for England.'

'But you accepted their conditions.'

'You can tell them that we shall be un-accepting unless they meet our suggestions.'

'It is no good, I cannot discuss these things. They are not my concern. You must write. Now will you please give me the money for the cheques and I must go.'

Bromley shook his head. 'No,' he said, blowing the word in her face. 'What's more you're not leaving until I say so.' He leaned back, looking pleased with himself. 'Since you mentioned "payment", let's start there. We pay too much for these cheques. We're the boys who run the risks; it's only right that headquarters should recognise the fact.'

'But this is nothing to do with me,' Freda exclaimed in an agitated voice. 'I know nothing about that side of things.'

'You will do if you just sit and listen.'

'I have to go,' she said with sudden determination. 'I cannot stay.'

She rose from her chair but Bromley put out a hand and pushed her gently back.

'And if headquarters think that we can be simply replaced by a more amenable bunch,' Bromley went on as though nothing had happened, 'then headquarters better have another think, because we shouldn't just sit idly by and watch others reap this particular harvest. No, it's us or no one, which means it's us, for I happen to know that they've made a nice little profit out of their English branch. And that puts us in a good bargaining position. Understand, Freda?'

For answer, Freda Fischer looked at her watch. 'I will tell what you have said when I get back,' she replied coldly, 'but I cannot guarantee that it will reach the right ears, because I do not know whose they are.'

'It'll reach the right ears all right,' Bromley said. 'Messages of this sort always do. However, I've not finished yet.'

'We have to work hard for our money, Freda,' Passfield broke in to George Bromley's obvious annoyance. 'It's not like robbing a mail train, two and half million for one night's work.'

Derek Armley sniggered. 'Robbing a mail train's easy by comparison.'

Freda turned on him. 'If it is so easy, why do you not do it, too?'

'Not enough mail trains to go round,' Passfield observed. This remark brought delighted laughter from Armley and Rutter, which was not, however, shared by Dayne, who sat impassively watching Freda, or by Bromley who was registering frowning displeasure at his temporary loss of control of the meeting.

'Just cut it out and leave me to do the talking,' he growled. Though none of them liked him, he nevertheless carried the necessary authority, so long as he remained their leader, to command attention.· Silence fell immediately and Passfield's face became a sulky mask once more.

'We'd like to handle more cheques and pay less for them,' Bromley said in a dangerously quiet voice. 'That's point one. And point two is that we're fed up with this elaborate front. We want it changed. Point three is that when I say *like* and *want*, I mean that's how it's going to be in future. Now that's the strength of the message you'll take back to headquarters. So far'—he glanced round at the others—'I've stuck to instructions and none of this lot even know the country you come from. But you can tell headquarters that I'm getting tired of communicating with a box number which appears to ignore my suggestions. Things have got to be changed—and changed to our liking.'

It was at this moment that Dayne sprang from his chair and shot across to the window. 'I'm almost sure I heard someone outside,' he said in a whisper as he peeped cautiously round the edge of the curtain.

In a second, Bromley was beside him. 'Out of the way, let me look,' he hissed. 'Yes, there is someone out there,' he said a moment later. 'Just over by the hedge. Now, who the bloody hell's snooping round here!' He let out a further ejaculation. 'There are two of them. My God and there's another.' He glanced back at the tense expressions now anxiously focused on him. 'Out quietly through the back way. Leave all the lights on. I'll take the suitcase. Call me at my place in the morning. You'll have to take your chance with the rest of us, Freda. There's no women and children first rule on this ship.' He took another quick look out of the window. 'It's the bloody police all right,' he said grimly. 'They're multiplying every minute, too.' Even as he turned back into the room, it was empty. The suitcase had also disappeared. He raced to the door. 'Give that to me, you . . .' He seized the case roughly from Rutter's hand as the latter was about to step out into the darkness. Ahead were shadowy figures dispersing like dandelion seed caught by a breeze.

All of a sudden a whistle blew from somewhere the other side of the bungalow and a voice shouted, 'Just all go back inside. You're surrounded and can't get away.'

There followed a sequence of confused sounds. Running feet, scuffling, more shouts mingled with a few grunts and the same voice, which had shouted, calling out further instructions to his followers.

In five minutes it was all over.

'Well, well, just look what we have here,' Detective-Superintendent Manton remarked as he gazed down at the neatly stacked piles of travellers cheques which filled the secret cavity of Freda's suitcase. Scattered on the floor beside the case lay its remaining contents. Manton bent down and picked up a pair of black lace panties. 'Really, George!' he exclaimed reprovingly. 'What will your wife say?'

Bromley's mouth hardened but he said nothing. Rutter, Armley, Dayne and Passfield remained as expressionless as blocks of salt, while half a dozen plain clothes officers stood behind them in an outer ring. More officers could be heard moving around outside.

'I believe you're the owner of this bungalow, aren't you, Rutter?' Manton asked.

'Tenant. Not owner.'

'Must be very pleasant here in the summer,' Manton observed. 'Keep a boat, do you?'

Rutter cast him an unamused smile.

'As soon as transport comes, we'll be away,' Manton went on.

An officer came into the room. 'We've searched the rest of the place, sir, but there doesn't seem to be anything else of significance.' He threw the five prisoners a curious and a slightly worried look. 'I wonder if I might have a word with you outside, sir.'

When Manton returned to the room five minutes later, he looked preoccupied.

'O.K., the van awaits,' he announced. He turned to the officer who had accompanied him into the room. 'Take them out singly, Jim. I'm not risking their bursting free outside like a rugger scrum. They'd better have bracelets on for the journey, too.'

The officer—Detective-Sergeant Jim Raikes—nodded. 'Right, Bromley, you first. Hands behind your back.'

With an officer fore and aft George Bromley was led out of the room. A couple of minutes later the procedure was repeated with Rutter: then with Passfield: then Armley, and finally with Dayne.

After the last departure, Manton remained alone in the room, his gaze roaming restlessly over the frippery furnishings. He looked up eagerly when Sergeant Raikes re-appeared in the doorway.

'Well?'

Raikes shook his head, while his expression depicted failure.

'No good, sir. Said it'd be more than his life would be worth.'

'What the hell are we going to do now?'

'Don't see what we can do, sir, except go ahead.'

'Who was the blithering idiot who caught him?'

'One of the uniform lads. He'd only just come off duty when he was roped in for this party and I suppose he wasn't given proper instructions. Not really his fault, sir. A bit of a box-up though.'

'That's a massive understatement,' Manton observed sourly. 'Oh, well, we'd better get back. Nothing more we can do here. Leave somebody to show the photographic and fingerprint people around when they arrive.' He nodded at the suitcase. 'Don't forget the luggage.'

11

Twenty minutes later the five prisoners were going through the process of being cautioned and charged and locked up for the night. Each had resisted the temptation to make any written statement or, indeed, to assist the police in any way. However, since they were caught with the goods on them, Manton, for his part, hadn't felt the same incentive to obtain statements as sometimes exists.

They were charged jointly with being in possession of forged travellers cheques, and the only one to make any reply in answer to the charge was George Bromley who said, 'If you think they're forged, prove it.'

To this, Manton had replied, 'Don't worry, I shall.'

Though the cells they occupied for the night were in a row, the dividing walls were solid and the opportunity of communication was nil. The thoughts of each, however, as he lay far from sleep, ran on similar lines and reached a similar conclusion. They had been well and truly shopped.

In an upstairs office of the station, a thick-set young man in a tweed jacket and regulation blue serge trousers stood in front of Manton's desk.

'I'm sorry, sir,' he said, though there was a note of defiance in his tone, 'but I wasn't told to let anyone through.'

Manton sighed heavily. 'Well, you realise what's happened. We've now got our informant charged and locked up.'

The young constable made a slight face. 'Couldn't he have been released, sir?'

'He could have, but he wouldn't go. He's a frightened man. Let him out now and the others will immediately know who grassed.'

'I suppose he'll just have to go through with it then. It's hardly my fault, sir, if I wasn't told.'

Not for the first time, Manton wondered what the force was coming to when a young constable could answer back quite so perkily, even if he was in the right. In the midst of his brooding, Detective-Sergeant Raikes came into the room.

'I've been delving a bit deeper into this mishap, sir.' Manton bit back the scalding comment which flew to his lips. The sergeant's euphemisms were really too much at a time such as this—'It seems it was the bloke's own fault. He must have lost his bearings in the darkness and he charged straight into P.C.

Cotter here, instead of slipping out through the gap in the hedge as arranged.'

'Did anyone try and escape through the gap in the hedge?' Manton asked.

'No, the chap there says not. Anyway, we caught all five of them, sir,' he added, with a faint note of surprise in his voice.

'I know we did. I was just wondering if there might have been a sixth we didn't know about.'

'No evidence of anyone else, sir,' Sergeant Raikes replied briskly.

'You didn't notice a faint smell of perfume in that room at the bungalow?'

Sergeant Raikes looked thoughtful for a moment, then shook his head. 'Can't say I did, sir. Fact is I have got a bit of a cold. I'll ask some of the others if you like, sir?'

'Yes. I'd like that checked.'

'We weren't expecting to find anyone else there, were we, sir?' Raikes asked in a faintly puzzled tone.

'No. But that doesn't rule out the possibility.'

There was a brief silence before Raikes said with a pleased grin, 'On the whole sir, I reckon we can count it a good evening's work. We've got enough to put them away for years and I haven't any doubt myself that we'll be able to tie this lot up with all the other forged travellers cheques which have been reported recently.'

'There are a good many evenings' work ahead of us before we'll be ready to proceed in court,' Manton said gloomily. 'I can see this enquiry branching out in more directions than a weather-vane before we're finished.'

After the two officers had left him, he rose from his chair and began to pace around the furniture. Twenty-five years' service had not provided him with any precedent for a situation in which a police informant becomes accidentally knocked off and then insists on being charged and proceeded against with his co-defendants.

Perhaps the first step was to see that he got a good lawyer. And by *good*, he meant one with whom the police were able to work without locking up all their papers every time he appeared.

Roger Elwin was the name which came immediately into his

mind. Roger Elwin, the junior partner in Rufford, Rich and Co., who handled all the firm's criminal work and who did a lot of prosecuting for the neighbouring county force.

Now he would be just the person to handle the somewhat ambiguous interests of Tony Dayne.

CHAPTER THREE

RITA BROMLEY stubbed out her half-smoked cigarette with a vicious gesture and leapt toward the telephone as soon as it began to ring.

'Is that you, Lew? What have you been able to find out?' Her voice was as hard as her face, though both now betrayed signs of the nervousness which had been consuming her since she had heard the news, soon after midnight, of what had befallen her husband. It was now half past seven, and though she had only lain on her bed for a few hours without sleep, she was heavily made-up and dressed in a tight black frock more appropriate to half past seven in the evening.

Lew Slater was the sort of brother one would have expected Rita Bromley to have, shrewd and vicious enough to silence the most determined do-gooder. His tone, as he now spoke, was urgent.

'Only that he's been charged and will be coming up in court this morning. We must have a lawyer there to get him bail. Leave that to me, Rita. I'll come round in an hour's time and pick you up. We'll try and see him before he goes over to court. It's next to the police station. So we'll call there first.'

'But what happened, Lew? What went wrong?'

'I don't know, Rita. I haven't been able to find out. The bloody police wouldn't tell me anything apart from the fact that George and the others have been charged with possessing forged cheques. We shan't know what happened until we see George. But don't worry, girl, they won't have George on the hook for long, he's too smart. See you in about an hour.'

Rita Bromley looked round the room, which was her notion of a film star's living-room, with an air of worried petulance. Eventually she rose from the white doeskin couch, on which she had been coiled, and fetched herself a brandy from the walnut and chrome bar at the foot of the short flying staircase which led by half a dozen steps to the only door in the room.

They had done well recently and George had given her her head in furnishing their new house. It had cost a packet, but she knew there was still plenty more where that had come from. No, it wasn't the thought of suddenly losing it all which worried her, since that was a negligible danger. It was simply the bleak prospect of a life without George, for whatever other failings Rita might have, disloyalty or unfaithfulness to her husband was not among them. She worshipped him. And he, in turn, indulged most of her expensive, and frequently garish whims with gruff good humour. And tacked on in a curious way to this picture of domestic harmony was her brother Lew. Lew lived alone. He had once been married, indeed still was in the eyes of the law, but he hadn't seen his wife for over ten years and had neither idea nor interest in what had happened to her. He was devoted to his sister and regarded his brother-in-law with dogged admiration.

Good as his word, he picked Rita up just as the eight-thirty news summary was beginning on the radio. The Bromley home was in Pinner, and it was a good half hour's drive round London's western perimeter to reach the police station where George and his confederates had spent the night.

'I want to see the officer who's dealing with the case of George Bromley,' Lew Slater announced to the officer in charge of the, enquiry desk.

'The detective-superintendent's looking after that one himself.'

'Tell him Mrs. Bromley and Mr. Slater want to see him.'

'He's pretty busy right now. What do you want to see him about?'

'We'll tell *him* that.'

'Are you the prisoner's wife?' the officer asked, looking across at Rita.

'I'm Mr. Bromley's wife,' she replied with dignity.

'O.K., just hang on a tick,' the officer said, and disappeared through a door behind him. In the inner office he used the station intercom to speak to Manton.

'Bromley's wife is here, sir. Wants to see you. She looks as though she's been put out of business by the Street Offences Act. She's got a nasty little runt with her, who looks as though someone has tried to chew off one of his ears. Will you see them? ... O.K. sir, I'll send them up.'

'This is Mrs. Bromley and I'm her brother,' Slater said when, a minute or two later, they were ushered through the door of Manton's office. 'Mrs. Bromley wants to see her husband.'

'If the Court agrees, she can do later, but not now. They'll probably let you both see him after the hearing—it'll only be a formal appearance as we're asking for a remand—before he's taken away to Brixton prison.'

'We'll be asking for bail,' Slater said nastily.

'No harm in asking, I suppose, but I shall certainly oppose the application.'

Slater frowned. 'We have Mr. Woodside coming. As you probably know, he's one of the top criminal lawyers in London. He'll see that George Bromley's rights are properly safeguarded.'

'Then you've nothing to worry about,' Manton observed. He turned to Rita. 'Seeing that you're here Mrs. Bromley, there are a few questions I'd like to ask you.'

'You've no right,' Slater broke in excitedly. 'You can't make her give evidence against her husband.'

'I know rather better than you do what I may or may not do. Perhaps you'd wait outside while I speak to Mrs. Bromley alone.'

Slater looked at his sister who said, 'It's O.K., Lew, I can look after myself. I'll join you in a minute or two.'

After her brother had made his reluctant departure, she said to Manton, 'What's your case against George?'

'Strong. He and the others were found with the goods on them.'

'Somebody must have grassed,' she said, carefully watching Manton's face as she spoke. When he remained silent, she added, 'Is that how you got on to them?'

'I didn't ask you to stay in order to ask me questions,' he replied.

'Nevertheless, just answer me this one. Are any further charges likely to be stuck on?'

'I should think it's more than possible that they'll be charged with a conspiracy of some sort.'

'I see.'

'Now let me ask you a few questions.'

She shook her head. 'I have nothing to say. I'm certainly not making any statement, so you might as well save your strength. You'll need it if you think you're going to keep George on the hook. You'll have to prove every word you utter and we shall be fighting you every inch of the way.' Throwing him a brittle smile, she crossed to the door. 'See you over in court, Superintendent.'

Manton stared ruefully out of the window for some minutes after she had gone. It was a long while since he had come up against a prisoner's wife quite as diamond hard as Rita. Any hope of gleaning a helpful lead from that source could be immediately discounted. Sometimes wives, albeit not competent witnesses against their husbands, provided useful background material for the police to work on. All he had got from Rita Bromley, however, had been an uncompromising challenge.

*   *   *

Manton felt oppressed as he walked over to court an hour or so later. Satisfaction over an undoubted coup was overshadowed by the hideous box-up which had resulted in Dayne's arrest. He could foresee endless complications over that, and was sure there were even worse ones which he couldn't at the moment foresee. The only consolation was that Dayne had agreed to instruct Messrs. Rufford, Rich and Co. in his defence, and that Roger Elwin had consented to take on the case.

He was in the lobby of the court-house when Manton entered.

'You sounded very mysterious on the 'phone,' he said, 'what's it all about?'

He was a young man in his latter twenties, bespectacled and with a head of rather boisterous curly hair, who displayed a like zest for everything he undertook, whether it was a law case, a game of hockey on a winter's afternoon or making love to Carol, who was his fiancée.

'Have you seen Dayne yet?' Manton asked.

Elwin shook his head. 'Thought I'd better have a word with you first.'

'I think it'd be better if you saw him, then if you come

17

across to the station after the hearing, I'll tell you all about things.'

Elwin gave a doubtful shrug. 'O.K., but you realise that a conflict of interest may arise. I shall be representing Dayne not the police.'

'You'll find that our interests coincide to a large extent.'

'We'll certainly discover whether that is so soon enough. How much am I supposed to know when I see him?'

'Just that the police are embarrassed by his presence behind bars and would like to find a way out of the dilemma.'

Roger Elwin grinned boyishly. 'It's not often one is given the opportunity of savouring police embarrassment.' He made a move to go. 'See you over the way afterwards then.'

'Are you Superintendent Manton?' a voice demanded on Manton's other side. 'My name's Woodside. I'm appearing for Mr. Bromley. Do I understand that you will be opposing bail?'

'Yes.'

'I can put up sureties.'

' 'Fraid not.'

Mr. Woodside, who had a slightly congested appearance, frowned.

'Well, you'd better know that we'll fight it right up to a judge in chambers if necessary.'

'I'll pass that information on,' Manton replied civilly.

To those who criticised the snail-like pace of legal process Manton had often reflected what an eye-opener it would be to observe the speed with which arrested men become legally, and often vociferously, represented.

When twenty minutes later his five prisoners trooped into the dock, each had a solicitor present. After Manton had given short evidence of arrest and said that he was asking for a week's remand in custody, Mr. Woodside rose to make his combative plea for bail. He was followed by Armley's solicitor who spoke of his client as he might have of a favourite pet about to be sent to kennels. The remaining three contented themselves with short formal applications. To no one's surprise, all were refused and the prisoners were led out, giving winks and small, confident smiles to friends and relations who filled the back of the court.

It was three quarters of an hour before Roger Elwin

knocked on the door of Manton's office and flopped into the only comfortable chair.

'Have a satisfactory interview with your chap?' Manton enquired.

'I'll answer that when you've told me what the whole thing is about.'

Manton leant back in his chair and stuck his legs out straight.

'Five days ago Dayne telephoned this station and spoke to one of my sergeants. He said he had some information of great interest to the police concerning the pushing of forged travellers cheques. He declined to give his name but he offered to meet my chap in a café about a couple of miles from here on the way to the airport and to produce, so to speak, some credentials. Well, my Sergeant—Raikes by the way, do you know him?'—Elwin nodded briefly—'went to the appointed place and there was Tony Dayne. First of all he produced a five-pound travellers cheque which he said was forged.'

'Was it?' Elwin broke in.

'Yes, and a very good forgery, too. Then he went on to tell Raikes that if he was interested in making a real haul he should arrange a raid on this bungalow—it's named Isola Capri by the way—not earlier than eight o'clock and not later than a quarter past on Wednesday evening. Last night, that is. And that he would not only find the loot, but the boys as well. Sergeant Raikes asked him who they were, but he refused to give their names on the grounds that we might be tempted to round them up piecemeal beforehand.'

'On what evidence?'

'Exactly. Sergeant Raikes pointed that out, but Dayne as adamant and still wouldn't give their names. I suppose he probably felt that he would have no aces left once he disclosed who they were, and decided to keep us on a lead.'

'But he told you how many you could expect to find?'

'Yes; five including himself.'

'And so a bargain was struck?' Elwin asked, with a glint in his eye.

'It was first of all suggested to him that he should stay right away from the bungalow, that he should think up some excuse for not being there, but he wouldn't hear of it.'

'I'm not really surprised.'

'I don't see why,' Manton retorted in a slightly nettled tone.

'Because it would have been obvious that it was he who had tipped you off.'

'I dare say it would, but we could have given him protection.'

'For twenty-four hours a day for the rest of his life?'

'Anyway, it's all academic since he insisted on being present. So then it was arranged that he should be allowed to escape through the net. There was bound to be a certain amount of confusion in the dark and nobody would think very much if one prisoner managed to get away. At all events,' Manton added crisply, 'your chap was satisfied with the arrangement.'

'And what was to happen to him afterwards?'

'I don't follow you.'

'You were really going to let him go for good?'

Manton looked hurt. 'When we strike a bargain of that sort, we stick to it. We'd be in a poor way without informants and whatever one may feel about them at large we respect their confidence.' Manton shifted in his chair. 'The rest you know. At the last minute we decided we'd better take a few extra bods along and unfortunately they—or one of them at any rate—weren't properly briefed, with the result that Dayne got nabbed. As soon as Sergeant Raikes told me what had happened, I decided that if the prisoners were taken out to the van separately, Dayne could be given a nudge and told to make a dash for it.'

'But he refused?'

'He refused,' Manton echoed glumly.

'Can't say I blame him,' Elwin commented. 'That, too, would have looked pretty suspicious.'

'Prisoners do manage to escape,' Manton replied.

'But only in circumstances which are either downright suspicious or which reveal startling negligence.'

'I couldn't have cared how negligent anyone thought I was if he'd got away.'

There was a short silence, then Elwin said, 'There's one thing you haven't told me, and that is the reason Dayne gave you for grassing.'

'He was simply a disgruntled member of the band. He thought the others, and Bromley in particular, had cheated

20

him and were proposing to do him further down over this present consignment of cheques.'

'Did he tell you where the cheques came from?'

Manton shook his head. 'We asked him that naturally, but he said Bromley was the only person who knew. They come in from somewhere abroad, but that was all he was able to say. And that was largely surmise, I gather.'

'He's small fry, in fact?'

'In the sense that they're all small fry apart from Big George. He was the boss and he wasn't one for sharing his secrets.'

Roger Elwin scratched the back of his head. 'Do you mean to say that until you caught this crowd, you had no idea who they were?'

'That's very nearly true. We'd naturally made a few enquiries and had discovered that the bungalow was rented to a man named Max Rutter. We'd also found out that Rutter and Bromley had recently been associating. Bromley is someone we've had on our books before and, indeed, I once arrested him myself about a dozen years ago. But that was all. We had no previous notion that this lot were tied up with the forged travellers cheques racket.' Manton gave the solicitor an appraising look. 'Does all this agree with what your client has already told you?'

'More or less,' Elwin replied vaguely. 'I haven't really had an opportunity of getting down to details with him yet.'

'What's his present feeling?'

'About being inside?' Manton nodded. 'He seems to think it's the safest place for him in the circumstances. He's adamant that nothing must be done which will arouse the others' suspicions.'

'What can you do for him?' Manton asked.

'Defend him to the best of my ability. What else?'·

'But supposing he's convicted and sent to prison, when we know all the time that he's got accidentally caught up in the machinery and shouldn't be in the dock at all?'

'I imagine there are ways and means of dealing with the situation. If the worst came to the worst, somebody could presumably let him out of the prison back door. The others wouldn't know anything about that if they were all in different prisons. Anyway, we're a long way off that stage.'

'I think I've told you the lot,' Manton said with a sigh. 'I'm personally grateful to you for taking on Dayne's defence, as you are one of the few people I could have told all I have. If there's anything you happen to learn from your client which you can properly pass back to me, I shall be further grateful.'

Roger Elwin rose. 'I'll go and see him in Brixton within the next few days. You've certainly provided me with a useful background, but I doubt whether I'm going to thank you very much for it. And heaven knows how I shall be able to string along with the other defending solicitors. I take it you don't want anyone to know what you've told me?'

'Not even Mr. Rufford or Mr. Rich,' Manton said with a smile.

'Mr. Rufford, peering down over the edge of his fleecy cloud, is doubtless already in the know. Mr. Rich, accompanied by the new Mrs. Rich, is holidaying in Marrakesh and could hardly be less interested if you broke all the Judges' Rules twenty times in one day.'

'One thing I'm particularly interested in finding out,' Manton said as the solicitor reached the door, 'is how a hundred thousand pounds' worth of forged travellers cheques arrived at the bungalow in a suitcase containing ladies clothing. Incidentally there was a car—a Fiat six hundred—parked there which belongs to Rutter. That was the only sign of transport.'

'Perhaps an examination of the clothing will assist you.'

'It hasn't so far, but the laboratory may be able to discover something.'

'No identifying tags or labels?'

'None.'

Elwin shrugged. 'Surely Bromley's the only person who can help you over that.'

'That means no help at all.'

'Despite having caught your prisoners red-handed, you really are in a bit of fix, aren't you!' Elwin observed cheerfully, and then bolted before Manton could reply.

CHAPTER FOUR

As Roger Elwin turned the key in his front door that evening he was greeted by the unmistakable smell of steak being grilled. This meant that Carol was already at work and that the steak would be edible, which it wasn't always if he was in charge, and that the salad would look less like hedge clippings than when he prepared it.

He lived in a small cottage just over the Surrey border and less than six miles from his suburban office. It had originally belonged to one of his firm's clients who had let it fall into a state of utter disrepair before announcing in a moment of bored indifference that he thought he might as well sell it. When Elwin had himself expressed interest, the client had said, through a yawn, he could have it for an entirely nominal sum if he really wanted it. That had been three years ago, since when it had been transformed by home labour into something of style and charm. There had scarcely been a weekend in which he hadn't added to its amenities in one way or another, and during the past six months he had been joined by Carol in the seemingly endless task of improvement.

Roger came from the north of England of a family who regarded those from London and the south as effete and unwarrantably stuck-up. He had been educated at the local grammar school and at one of the northern Redbrick universities. It was in the north, too, that he had served his articles and become qualified as a solicitor. And then by one of those accidents which so often set one's life off on a different course, he had almost suddenly found himself with Messrs. Rufford, Rich and Co. who operated from three offices on London's western perimeter. It so happened that the firm was looking for young blood at the time and had been impressed by Roger's handling, on behalf of his old firm, of a mutual transaction, and a discreet feeler was put out. Roger, who nurtured none of his family loyalties toward the north, jumped at the opportunity, and within a month had moved. A year later Mr. Rufford had died and not long after that Mr. Rich, a widower, married a flighty new wife. These two events tended to accelerate Roger's promotion in the firm, and nine months ago he had been given a junior partnership. It was on the evening he had been celebrating this event that he had met Carol Chant.

She was five years younger than him and a secretary with a firm of architects in the West End. She lived with her parents not far from Roger's cottage, her father being a local bank manager.

Roger dropped his briefcase on the chair in the tiny hall and pushed open the kitchen door.

'Hello, darling,' he said happily at the preoccupied figure by the stove.

'Oh, you made me jump. I never heard you come in.'

Carol turned in time to receive his kiss.

'I'm so glad you're here. You must have got away earlier than you expected.'

'I did. Mr. Arkwright had a headache and went home just after four and to my surprise said I might as well leave, too.'

'Pity Mr. Arkwright doesn't have more headaches. Had a drink, darling?'

'No, I waited for you.'

'What?'

'Could you make a dry martini?'

'Excellent choice.'

'I know you always enjoy doing them.'

'Because I do them so well,' he replied affably as he retired to the living-room where the bottles were kept.

As he set about making the martini, it occurred to him not for the first time that during the past few months he had certainly been enjoying the best of both worlds. The life of a bachelor, with many of the pleasures of marriage, though without the complications and responsibilities of its legal status.

He realised that this state of affairs could not be perpetuated, if only because Carol would sooner or later reach a stage of rebellion, and, indeed, to do himself justice he didn't wish it himself. But it had its attractions while it lasted.

'Here you are, love,' he said, handing her an ice-cold glass of the subtlest concoction any barman has devised. He sipped his own. 'A dry martini's like a soufflé or a pancake, it must be ingested immediately otherwise it loses its magic.'

'What on earth does *ingested* mean?'

'Taken into the body.'

'Sounds a typical lawyer's word.'

'As far as I know it has nothing to do with the law whatsoever. It's a perfectly ordinary word . . .'

'Well, if you'll just get out some knives and forks, we'll ingest these steaks,' Carol broke in. Roger did as he was bidden. 'Do you have to work this evening?' she asked after they had sat down.

'I should do a little.'

'That's O.K. I only wondered if you wanted me out of the way immediately.'

'Not before you've done the washing-up,' he said sternly, and let out an exclamation as Carol kicked him vigorously on the shin.

'Have you seen Matthew this evening?' he asked suddenly, looking round the kitchen.

'He was on the roof when I came.'

Matthew was a large short-haired blue persian, who gave every sign of thinking that the cottage was run entirely for his benefit. As an occasional token of gratitude he would leave some portion of dead prey outside Roger's bedroom door.

Roger finished his last mouthful. 'That was delicious, darling. The inner man is satisfied.' He wiped his mouth. 'Now let me tell you about a case I've got involved in to-day. Not to be repeated by the way.'

Carol listened attentively. When he reached the end, she asked, 'Do the police often strike bargains with criminals?'

'I don't rightly know, but I imagine it happens from time to time. After all, a good deal of their most useful information in the detection of crime must come from extremely dubious sources. When I say *dubious* I don't mean necessarily unreliable. But it's not an aspect of their work that is usually revealed to the public or even to the judge or lawyers concerned in the particular case. "On information received," they say, and it's kept at that.'

'But if this Tony Dayne helped the police, how can he be guilty? He was sort of on their side all the time.'

Roger nodded enthusiastically. 'It's quite a legal conundrum and you've put your finger on the vital point in one. Namely, can Dayne be said to have had any *mens rea*, i.e., a guilty mind? If he didn't, then he can't be convicted of any offence.'

'That's wonderful, Roger.'

'It would be except that it's the last thing he can admit in open court in front of his co-defendants.'

'Then what are you going to do?'

'I've no idea at the moment. I'll go and see him in prison to-morrow, and I may then have a clearer notion, though I doubt it.'

'I must say,' Carol remarked thoughtfully, 'that I find it hard to feel much sympathy for your client. It was a pretty poisonous thing to do, to grass on all your associates, however badly they may have treated you.'

'A very natural emotional reaction.'

'His or mine?'

'Yours, but it doesn't help solve my problem.'

'What sort of person is he?'

Roger appeared thoughtful for a few seconds. 'He wasn't too happy when I saw him this morning, but I'd think he was normally rather an amiable character. He's small, not exactly insignificant looking but without anything in particular which strikes the eye or mind.' After a pause, he added, 'I can imagine he might excite your maternal instinct.'

Carol made a face. 'Usually the males of whom other men say that resemble retarded hamsters.'

'There's nothing retarded about Master Dayne, though come to think of it he's not unlike a hamster. He certainly has the same bright-eyedness.'

Carol's own eyes suddenly shone with excitement. 'Why don't we drive over and look at the bungalow now? I've never been to the scene of a crime before.'

'O.K., but we shan't be able to go in.'

'We might be able to.'

Roger assumed an air of extended forbearance. 'In the first place the police will have sealed it. In the second we'd be trespassers. And in the third . . .'

'Let's go, anyway,' Carol interrupted.

They twice had to ask the way, and when they did arrive outside 'Isola Capri' it was to observe nothing more than a squat outline.

'There, I told you there'd be nothing to see,' Roger said.

'You didn't say anything of the sort. Anyway, surely we're going to get out of the car?'

'Of course.'

A second or two later they stood at the wicket gate which bore a home-painted inscription 'Isola Capri'. The bungalow itself was set well back from the road and was half hidden from view by an overgrowth of shrubs.

'Clearly there wasn't a gardener among them,' Roger remarked as they stepped inside the gate. 'Tidying up this place would be tougher than giving a Beatle a haircut.'

'It's spooky,' Carol said, slipping her hand into his. 'Do you think we ought to go any closer?'

'Yes, now we're here, let's case the joint.' They moved along the path toward the bungalow. 'The noise here last night must have sounded like a herd of elephants crashing about in jungle.'

They reached the front door and Roger tried the handle. As he had expected, it was locked. 'Come on, let's walk round and see what lies at the back.'

Occasionally tripping and stumbling, they made their way to the rear of the bungalow where there was a small rough lawn and beyond it an overgrown orchard.

'Garage must be the other side,' Roger muttered as they continued their way. About fifteen yards on the farther side they burst through a tangle of overgrown lilac bushes to find themselves on a grass track which was a veritable tunnel through the greenery and which led back to the road. 'I suppose this is where the police found the car,' he said, peering about him less futilely now that his eyes had become accustomed to the dark. 'I wonder which my chap's escape route was meant to be.'

'How many men did the police have?' Carol asked.

'Manton didn't say. Only that at the last minute they decided to bring along an additional one or two.'

'He must rather regret that he did now.'

Roger chuckled. 'It certainly was an unkind twist which led to increased precaution wrecking the plan.' They emerged on to the road. 'Feel any different, love, now you've visited the scene of a crime?'

'It's more like the setting for a murder,' Carol said, clutching his hand a bit tighter.

'Don't try and complicate things,' he replied, turning his head to kiss her. For a few seconds they were aware only of each other, then in the warm after-glow of their embrace they strolled slowly back toward the car. As they reached it, Roger said, 'I wonder what the truth really is.'

'Don't you believe what the police told you?'

'Yes, I believe them all right—at least I think I do—but how much do they really know?'

'You'll probably learn a lot more when you have a proper talk with Dayne in prison.'

'It's possible.' His tone, however, was even less sanguine than his words. 'But it certainly won't be for want of trying. Apart from purely professional interest, I'm intrigued by the whole set-up.' He grinned happily at Carol. 'The law really is a fascinating occupation and to think my mother wanted me to become a bishop! I'd never have met you or Dayne.'

CHAPTER FIVE

EXERCISE at Brixton prison was taken twice a day and consisted of an aimless shuffle round an oval circuit under the bored eyes of a couple of prison officers. It did, however, even if it fell short of keeping anyone's muscles in trim, afford an opportunity for talk.

Prisoners normally kept in twos and threes, and were able to drop back to rejoin another group or quicken their pace to catch up the one in front. Only a few preferred to walk alone in a morose silence.

On the afternoon following their remand in custody, Dayne and Passfield had paired off and were walking several yards behind Bromley, Rutter and Armley.

Passfield, who was undoubtedly the most emotional member of the gang, was sunk in a deep depression.

'We're going to get ten years at least,' he said in bitter self-pity.

'We haven't been convicted yet,' Dayne replied.

'Caught red-handed with the cheques almost sticking to our fingers, what hope have we got!' He lowered his voice, 'I'll tell you what I believe, Tony, it's that Big George has something to do with our being grabbed.'

'How could he have?' Dayne asked in a startled tone. 'After all, he's here, too.'

'I mean I think he opened his big mouth too wide and the police got a whiff of what was on. I wouldn't put it beyond that wife of his, or her precious brother, to have talked too much.'

'Do you have any evidence for saying that?' Dayne asked keenly.

Passfield shook his head. 'Just a hunch. What's your theory, Tony?'

'Much the same as yours,' Dayne said. 'I've never trusted Rita, still less Lew Slater.'

'But you're not suggesting that they deliberately shopped us?' Passfield asked.

Dayne shrugged. 'Deliberate or not, the result's been the same.'

For a while they walked in silence. Then Passfield said, 'What are we going to do about it?'

'Better sound the others before we decide anything,' Dayne replied cautiously. He had noticed Bromley look over his shoulder and had guessed that he was about to drop back and join them. This he now did, slowing down until Dayne and Passfield drew level with him.

'Enjoying the walk, Tony? Roy?' he enquired with a pretence at a smile. Neither of them made any reply but waited for him to go on. 'Either of you any idea what happened to Freda?' he asked without further preliminary.

'I imagine she's now back where she came from,' Dayne remarked. 'She was the lucky one.'

'Lucky?' Bromley enquired.

'They may have caught her,' Passfield said. 'This isn't yet a mixed prison. So how do we know?'

'We know she wasn't caught with the rest of us,' Bromley said in a squashing tone. 'And that being so, how would the bloody police even know of her existence?' He shot Passfield a suspicious glance. 'Eh? How would they?'

'They seem to have known enough, why not a bit more?' Passfield demanded sourly.

'No, I guess Tony's right and she got right away.'

Dayne nodded thoughtfully. 'Which means we can't expect any help from that quarter; or can we, George? You're the one who'd know.'

'I doubt it,' Bromley said in a vague tone, which seemed to

29

indicate to the other two that he might know less than he was prepared to admit.

'What was the last you saw of her, Roy?'

'I never saw her at all after I got out of the room,' Passfield said. 'I wasn't interested in anyone, except myself. And I don't mind admitting it.'

'What about you, Tony? Derek says you were just behind her.'

Dayne, who had appeared about to answer the question, checked himself as Bromley added what could be considered an admonition to truth.

'Yes, that's right, I was,' he said. 'She shot away into the bushes to the left. I did, too, but I never saw her again.'

'Do you mean toward the grass track?' Dayne nodded. 'She must have got into the next-door garden and out that way into the other road.'

'But there's a fence between the track and the garden next door,' Dayne remarked. 'There's scarcely space for a dog to squeeze through.'

'Nevertheless, that's the way she must have gone,' Bromley said. 'You confirm what I'd begun to suspect.' He looked at them as they continued their shuffle. 'Don't you see it? It must have been Freda who grassed.'

'Freda?' Dayne echoed incredulously. 'But she was only a courier. Why should she have grassed?'

'That's exactly what I intend to find out,' Bromley said grimly. 'But if five people are neatly caught and the sixth slips away, by my reckoning the sixth has a bit of explaining to do.'

'She might just as well be on the moon for all the explaining we can get her to do,' Passfield observed.

'Don't be so sure,' Bromley said. 'I just wanted confirmation of the direction she took and you've given it me, Tony.'

'But I still don't see how you think she got through the fence,' Dayne said in a puzzled tone.

'If somebody wanted her to get through it, she'd get through it. Follow?'

'You mean the police cut a hole in it or something like that?'

'Exactly.'

'It still sounds far-fetched to me. What do you think, Roy?'

'All I know is that I'd be happy to put a bullet into the guts of whoever it was who landed us here.' He turned to Bromley. 'We've been content to accept your leadership, George, and not ask unnecessary questions, but I think it's time you told us a bit more. After all,' he added unpleasantly, 'some of us may be thinking it's your fault we're here. If we'd known more, this situation might have been avoided.'

'It wouldn't,' Bromley replied brusquely. 'Somebody grassed and that somebody must have been Freda.'

'For a start, tell us where she came from,' Dayne said.

Bromley appeared to be thinking hard, a process which, in his case, was slow but usually produced decisions.

'Vienna,' he said after a long pause.

'City of my dreams!' Passfield mimicked, and then in a savage tone added, 'And what does the little bitch do in Vienna when she's not trotting round Europe delivering forged travellers cheques?'

Bromley glanced at him with distaste. 'I don't know what she does.'

'And how much more do you know of what goes on there?' Dayne asked.

'Nothing.'

'Are you saying that little Freda just finds the pretty cheques on the banks of the Danube and plucks them like wild flowers?' Passfield enquired in a withering tone.

'I'm saying that I've had just about enough of your grue-some wit,' Bromley remarked.

'Yes, stop being waspish, Roy,' Dayne broke in. 'Go on, George, what's the rest of the set-up in Vienna?'

'As far as I'm concerned, it's no more than a post office box number.'

'What is the box number?' Passfield asked.

Bromley winked at Tony Dayne before replying blandly, 'I've forgotten.'

'What do Max and Derek think?' Dayne asked.

'Same as I do.' There was a silence, and they completed a further half-circuit before Bromley said, 'The important thing is to close our ranks and do nothing which can help the police. They'll have to prove every word they put into the charge. As far as our solicitors are concerned, we tell them that we'd gone to the bungalow to spend the evening with Max, to have a nice little game of cards and that we know absolutely nothing about any travellers' cheques. Luckily we hadn't opened the suitcase before the police dropped in.'

'But what's Max going to say to account for its presence in the bungalow?' Dayne asked.

'His defence will be that a man he's met a couple of times, but no more, on hearing that he lived near the airport asked if he might leave a suitcase with him while he was abroad. Told Max that he would pick it up on his return to England in a fortnight's time.'

'What's the name of Max's acquaintance?' Dayne enquired.

'Carmelo Bastani. He's a foreigner.'

'You surprise me!' Passfield observed.

'Isn't anyone going to think it curious that Max agreed to perform this little service for a relative stranger?' Dayne asked anxiously.

'Not if it's put over well and we can trust Max to do that. The further beauty of the story is that it opens up for a jury all sorts of exciting speculation.' Bromley grinned knowingly. 'Isn't Carmelo Bastani just the type of person you'd expect to find dealing in forged travellers cheques?'

'What's the chance of the police getting on to our travel agency lark?'

'We'll just have to keep our fingers crossed. Time won't be on their side as our lawyers will be prodding them to get on with the case, and it'll require time before they can dig up the whole story. Not only time, they'd also have to find people who would be able to recognise us.'

'Charming for Tony and me!' Passfield remarked. 'We're the only two who ever had dealings with the public.'

'Then you'd better start growing your hair differently,' Bromley replied in an unsympathetic voice. 'But time is the real element on our side. We must push the police into presenting the case as soon as possible. If they're not ready, then we'll make them let us out on bail which'll be even better.' He glanced from Dayne to Passfield. 'Now are you genned up on what you have to say to your lawyers? Naturally they'll be getting together and comparing notes, but they can only work on what we tell them, so make it good.'

As he finished speaking he quickened his pace to rejoin Rutter and Armley. A couple of minutes later exercise finished, and they were returned to their cells.

Dayne hadn't long been in his when the door was unlocked and a prison officer said laconically, 'Come.'

Their journey through the block and across the yard was in silence. Dayne's escort looked as bored as he was uncommunicative, but Dayne realised from the direction they were taking that the interview block was their destination. This was a low one-storey building close to the administrative block and consisted of a row of small, cheerless rooms, which had a generally dispiriting effect on visitor and visited alike.

Roger Elwin was mentally composing a caustic letter to the Home Secretary about the depressing state of amenities for lawyers visiting clients in Her Majesty's prisons when Dayne was ushered in.

'Afternoon, Mr. Elwin,' he said, 'I wasn't expecting to see you so soon. Something happened?'

Roger shook his head. 'I just thought that the sooner I know where we stand the better.'

'Sure,' Dayne replied, a slight note of wariness in his tone.

'In the first place, are you still determined to go through with this?'

'I haven't any choice, Mr. Elwin.'

'The police seem to be genuinely embarrassed by your presence inside.'

Dayne gave a mirthless laugh. 'I don't know how that's supposed to leave me. I'm not embarrassed, I'm just bloody frustrated. But I'd sooner be that than decorating a mortuary slab.'

'Are you sure that you would be if the police found some pretext to let you out?'

'I'm darned certain of it.' He leaned forward and said earnestly, 'Look, Mr. Elwin, life isn't as sacred in my sort of circle as it probably is in yours. People who grass don't just run a risk which passes in a few days, it's with them for all time. If Big George—that's Bromley—ever began to think that it was I who grassed, I'm telling you my life wouldn't be worth that.' He snapped his fingers with the sound of a whip being cracked. 'I shouldn't see my thirtieth birthday, and it's not all that far off.'

Roger pursed his lips and said, 'But the fact remains that

33

you did grass and I don't see why your life should be in much greater danger if you were to be freed now than if the plan had gone properly and you had got away at the time. Surely that would have aroused their suspicions?'

'Not if I'd played my cards properly afterwards and rallied round behind the scenes. They'd have accepted that in the scramble we each had a chance to escape and that I was the lucky one.' An impudent grin crossed his face. 'After all I'm the smallest and most athletic of the bunch and, if anyone could have got through the cordon, I could.' His expression became abruptly solemn. 'But now, as far as they're concerned, I was caught red-handed with them and there's no reason why I should receive any different treatment from the rest of them. And if any of them got an idea that I was being treated differently, it'd start them thinking immediately. And they wouldn't be nice thoughts either, Mr. Elwin.'

'Is Bromley the one you're most afraid of?'

'He and Armley are the most dangerous. Neither of them would lose any sleep if they killed a man. They might even go out and celebrate.' There was silence for a few seconds, then Dayne went on, 'The police bungled and I'm the loser, but I'm also their responsibility and I'm not going to have myself made a sacrifice just to help remove the blushes from their faces. I'd sooner do ten years inside than have any obvious punches pulled and be released now.'

'Right,' Roger said with an air of finality, 'there doesn't seem to be anything further to say on that score for the time being. Do you want to tell me how the suitcase of forged cheques reached the bungalow?'

'All I knew was that they'd be there that evening.'

'Who brought them?'

Dayne looked thoughtful and Roger could see that he was carefully weighing his answer.

'You'd better ask Bromley that question. He was the boss.' His tone became scornful. 'He liked to keep the details to himself and to treat the rest of us like kids. The fact is that he was a big chiseller. He doesn't know how to play straight with anyone.'

'Is that why you grassed?'

'Sure it is.'

'What did you hope to gain out of it?'

34

'I just wanted the satisfaction of putting him where he belonged.'

'And the other three as well?'

Dayne made a derisive noise with his lips. 'You trying to appeal to my better nature, Mr. Elwin? If I hadn't shopped them, they were going to do me.'

'They?'

'Bromley and Armley for certain and Rutter was probably in it, too.'

'What do you mean by "do" you?'

'Drop me overboard.'

'Why?'

'Bromley didn't like me. And anything he said was good enough for the other two.'

'If he didn't like you why did he enlist you in the first place?'

'Because I had the know-how he was looking for. I'd once worked in a travel agency. I knew the jargon.'

'Do you have evidence that Bromley was preparing to discard you?'

'Not your sort of lawyer's evidence, but enough for me.'

'And if they had done so, wouldn't they have been afraid that you would shop them out of spite?'

'They'd have reckoned I'd have been too scared.' A sly look came into Dayne's eyes. 'You see, Mr. Elwin, it all comes back to what's obvious and what isn't. If I'd got away as I was meant to the other evening, that wouldn't have been obvious. But supposing I'd sent a message saying I had a nasty cold and wouldn't be coming along and then the police had strolled in and collected them, that would have been obvious. Similarly it would be obvious if I was to be let out now while they're all kept inside. Get it? And believe me, Mr. Elwin, there's nothing as obvious as a bullet hole between the eyes.'

Roger smiled wryly. 'Anything else you'd like to tell me before I go?'

'I suppose I'd better tell you what our defence is,' Dayne said lightly and proceeded to give his solicitor details of his and Passfield's recent conversation with Bromley. When he had finished, he remarked, 'There's no problem about going along with the others on that, is there?'

'Your whole defence presents one enormous ethical problem,' Roger replied with feeling. 'Don't you see that?'

'I don't know what's ethical about it.' Dayne sounded petulant. 'Where do ethics come in?'

'Taking part in what one knows to be a charade.'

'Whose fault is that?'

'I daresay it's not yours, but that doesn't alter the position. As a solicitor, I'm bound by a certain code of conduct. I don't want to sound stuffy, but there are certain courses I couldn't lend myself to. I couldn't, for example, put forward a defence on your behalf which I knew to be untrue because you had told me so.'

Dayne looked sceptical. 'I thought it went on all the time. Anyway, isn't part of your job to tell me what to say?'

'It certainly is not,' Roger replied indignantly. 'Some solicitors may guide their clients a bit more than others, but it is the solicitor who takes instructions from his client and not the other way about.' He sighed. 'However, we needn't go into the ethics of my profession at the moment.'

'It was you brought it up.'

'I know; and it's something I shall have to resolve.'

Dayne looked up sharply. 'Look, Mr. Elwin, I'm in enough trouble as it is, I don't want to find myself in any worse just because your conscience decided to play up.'

'Don't worry, that won't happen.'

'Well, I am worried. First the police make a mess of things, then my lawyer shows signs of melting round the edges. What do you expect me to be?'

'I'm sorry,' Roger said in a contrite tone. 'I promise you that I shan't do anything to make your lot any worse.'

'I was hoping you'd be able to do something to make it a great deal better,' Dayne replied in a disgruntled voice.

'I hope I shall, too.' Roger wished he had never mentioned the question of ethics. It was not only a silly thing to have brought up with Dayne, but, as he now recognised, an unfair one as well. This was not to say, however, that a very real ethical problem didn't remain. It did, though perhaps there was hope that events would help to solve it. 'Do you have any family or friends you want me to get in touch with?' he asked, after a pause.

Dayne looked surprised. 'No thanks.'

'Nobody at all?'

'Nobody at all.'

'You're not married?'

Dayne shook his head. 'Not now, and never have been.'

'Parents alive?'

'Father is, I think. At least he was last time I heard of him a couple of years back. My mother died when I was a kid.'

'Brothers or sisters?'

'What do you want to know all this for?' he asked suspiciously.

'Frankly, out of curiosity,' Roger replied with a disarming smile.

'I've got some step-brothers and sisters, but I've not seen any of them for over five years. I certainly don't want any of them sticking their noses into my life now.'

'They may do, anyway, if they read your name in the papers.'

'I doubt it.' He stared frowningly at the table, then suddenly looking up went on, 'Don't think me rude, Mr. Elwin, but I'd prefer you shouldn't enquire beyond what I've already told you. It's not going to help you with my case and . . . well, I just prefer you didn't.'

Shortly after the interview was concluded. As Roger made his way toward the main gate, he was passed by a man and woman who he recognised from having seen them in court the previous day. It was later that he learnt they were Bromley's wife and brother-in-law.

All the way back to the office—a hideous drive through South London's cross traffic—he pondered the case. And the more he did so the less he liked it as a lawyer and the more it intrigued him as a person.

There was something admirably self-contained about Tony Dayne and yet he didn't add up to a whole person. Interviewing him had been like doing a jigsaw puzzle and reaching the end only to discover that several important pieces are missing.

But it wasn't merely Dayne, but everyone concerned in the case, whose conduct was permeated with a quality of dreamlike unreality. And that went for the police as well.

CHAPTER SIX

IN the course of her escape Freda Fischer had ripped a stocking and the heel of her left shoe had become loose. For forty-five minutes she had crouched, shivering and uncomfortable, against the farther hedge in the garden next to 'Isola Capri'. It wasn't until all was again silent next door and the last police car had departed that she cautiously emerged.

Though still frightened and shaken by her experience, not least by the hair-breadth nature of her escape, the three quarters of an hour spent cowering in the edge had provided her with an opportunity to review her plight and reach some sort of a decision.

It had, before things went wrong, been her intention to spend the night in one of the new airport hotels and fly back to Vienna the next morning. Now, dishevelled as she was and without any luggage, it would be inviting attention to enter a hotel. Luckily, she did have her handbag, containing her passport and return ticket.

Before leaving the cover of the neighbouring garden, she decided to remove her stockings. Bare legs, even in March and even if noticed, were less likely to excite interest than one heavily torn stocking which looked like an exhibit in a rape case.

The mist was patchy and as such doubly welcome. It provided some cover to her movement, but wasn't so thick as to have grounded aircraft. She could hear them tantalisingly close overhead. If only one could lower her a rope and fly her straight home.

With the heel of her shoe loose, walking was made brutally uncomfortable and several times she was forced to stop and, indeed, almost to give up in sobbing despair. On each occasion, however, realisation of the alternative drove her on.

At last she reached a main road and with untold relief saw that it was also a bus route. There was a stop about a hundred yards along, and she made her way toward it with the single-minded determination of a desert-traveller espying an oasis. The shelter beside it was deserted and she gratefully sat down to wait.

A car drove slowly past and disappeared from her view. A

few seconds later, however, it backed into sight again and the passenger door swung open to reveal an empty seat.

'Hello, there, want a lift?' The voice was superficially friendly, the face behind it wore a quizzical smirk.

'Where to?' she asked cautiously.

'That's a good question,' the voice said cheerfully. 'Where'd you like to go?'

'I'm waiting for a bus.' Her tone conveyed a rebuff, which was lost on the driver of the car.

'Cold, unfriendly things, buses. Anyway there won't be another.'

'There will be one in five minutes. I have seen the schedule there.' She pointed at the concrete post on which the times of the service were advertised.

'Come on, jump in. I'll drive you where you want.'

'No, thank you.'

'Where you from?'

'I don't understand.'

'You're not English. What country do you come from?'

'I do not wish to speak further.'

'What's wrong with you?' The voice still held its ingratiating note. 'Surely you're not frightened of men at your age? How old are you, by the way? No, don't tell me, I'll guess.' He leaned farther over from the driver's seat so that his head was out of the passenger door. 'I'd say you were twenty-seven or eight. Right?'

'No. Please go away and leave me.'

'That wouldn't be very chivalrous. It's not very nice for a girl to be alone in a bus shelter late at night.' He beamed an ogling grin at her. 'I'd never forgive myself if I were to read in the papers tomorrow that something horrid had happened to a girl at this very spot.'

Freda looked around her desperately. If necessary, she'd make a dash for it. The engine of his car was still running and she'd be able to get a little distance before he could give chase. He was obviously a sex maniac, there was a crocodile glitter about his eyes which proclaimed abnormality. From all she had heard, England was full of such.

'I shall scream if you don't leave me alone,' she said loudly.

The grin on his face became set like a waxwork mask.

'I can see you're one of those who likes a bit of rough treatment. Well, that's O.K. by me, I'm ready to oblige.' His tone had become harsh and determined.

Suddenly Freda gave a small gasp of relief as round the bend of the road swung a large, friendly bus. She dashed out of the shelter waving her arms at it frantically for fear the driver shouldn't notice her presence. It pulled up immediately behind the car and she was aboard before her tormentor had taken in the situation. Seconds later, however, the passenger door was slammed and the car pulled away in a burst of protesting sound.

There was only one other passenger on the lower deck of the bus, and Freda chose a front seat where her face would be less noticed than if she sat near the exit.

Her mind was filled now with a single thought. To get out of England as quickly as possible. It had suddenly become a symbol of nightmare disaster which would remain with her for life.

The conductor, who was coloured, looked tired. He obviously had little interest in his passengers other than the formal collection of their fares, and was set on reaching the end of the run and his own home with the minimum of fuss.

Freda tendered half a crown and looked pointedly to her front.

'Where to?' The conductor asked wearily.

'Near the airport, please.'

'We don't pass it on this route.'

Freda nodded as though she already knew this, though in fact her heart sunk a little farther at the news. She had hoped the bus might let her down outside the main entrance.

'To Henlys corner then?' he enquired.

She nodded again and he presented her with a ticket and a shilling change, before dragging himself back to the platform at the rear. When a quarter of an hour later, she left the bus, he appeared to be asleep even though his eyes were still open.

Her one consolation now was that she knew her whereabouts, which was two miles from the airport on the London side. Sore and blistered though her one heel was, it would be better to walk it than risk further encounters with prowling males by waiting at a bus stop. At least the road had houses on each side, and there were also one or two all-night garages which she remembered passing on a previous occasion when she had departed in the small hours. These should be an insurance against a repetition of her earlier encounter.

By the time she arrived at the airport, she had decided that her first act must be to discover the time of the next flight to Vienna. It would be risky to present herself at the ticket counter until there was a plane about to leave. A lone girl arriving at the airport in the middle of the night without either baggage or any clear idea of when a plane left for her destination would certainly be remembered if any questions were later asked. She would also have to account for her absence of baggage.

It seemed as though luck had turned her way when she found that there was a night flight leaving in an hour's time. Moreover, it was an Austrian Airlines flight which meant that she would feel secure as soon as she stepped aboard. To fly in a British 'plane would be to prolong the terrifying sense of uneasiness.

She held her breath while the counter clerk studied a list and then made a 'phone call to check that there was space on the aircraft.

'Yes, Miss Fischer, that'll be all right,' she said, tearing out the flight coupon. 'Would you put your bags on to the scale, please?'

'I haven't a bag. It was stolen.'

The girl behind the counter, who was trim and dark and the freshest-looking person within sight at a quarter past midnight, glanced up from the label she was endorsing.

'Here at the airport do you mean?'

'No, in London. I left it on the pavement while I went to look for a taxi and when I turned round it had gone.'

The clerk tossed her head. 'I don't know what this country's coming to. Our standards of honesty are worse than an oriental bazaar. You've reported it to the police?' Freda nodded. 'I'm afraid there's not much hope of your ever seeing it again. I hope you're insured?' Freda nodded again. 'That's some consolation then, but what a disagreeable experience. I only hope it won't put you off returning to England one day.' Her eye drifted to the ticket which lay on the desk in front of her and a small frown gathered on her brow.

'According to this, you only arrived in the country a few hours ago. And now you're going back to Vienna?'

Freda swallowed. 'It is all a lot of accidents,' she said in a tone which she had no difficulty in making sound pathetic. 'When I arrive, there is a message saying my father is suddenly very ill and then I have my case stolen.'

'You certainly have had bad luck.' She handed Freda a boarding pass. 'Anyway, I hope you'll find your father better by the time you reach home.'

'Thank you.'

'And may your next trip to England be a much happier one.'

'I hope so,' Freda said, and meant it.

The immigration officer, who stamped her passport, studied her as though she were a volunteer for the gas chamber but said nothing. Half an hour later, the lights below had been abruptly extinguished by a layer of cloud, and Freda for the first time set to thinking how she was going to explain things when she got back. It suddenly came home to her that the task of doing this was going to be even less enviable than the experience she had recently endured.

Though she might know rather more about what went on at headquarters than she was prepared to admit to George Bromley and his associates, this wouldn't make her task any lighter. Plans had gone woefully wrong and she had no illusions about being accorded a heroine's return. People who lived by international crime were not often moved by sentiment.

Freda lay back in her seat and a shiver ran through her body.

CHAPTER SEVEN

IT was routine rather than optimism which prompted Manton to apply for a warrant to search Bromley's home. It was unlikely that he would come across anything of interest, but even an outside chance justified the course being taken.

In the two days since the arrests, enough (though in another sense, not enough) had happened for him to realise that this was one of those cases in which he would shortly have everyone upon his back. It invariably happened when an arrest was made and the acquisition of evidence followed.

It's one thing to grab five men gloating over a suitcase of forged cheques, another to prove all the links necessary to show what was going on. Moreover, he was acutely aware in the cold light of day that when the police had made their haul, the suitcase was still demurely closed, so that Bromley and his friends could deny knowledge of its contents. An unlikely story, perhaps, but you never knew with a jury, especially if you weren't able to fill in more of the picture for them. His superiors had already begun to show signs of nail-biting fret over what had happened with Dayne, and it wouldn't be long before the lawyers on both sides started to snipe at him.

Accordingly, he was in a sombre frame of mind as, with Detective-Sergeant Raikes, he drove over to the Bromley home in Pinner armed with his search warrant.

'I've been investigating the possibility of there having been someone else in the bungalow that evening, sir,' Sergeant Raikes said as he braked the car to a halt at traffic lights.

'Any luck?'

'None. So far there are no unaccountable fingerprints. None that are identifiable, that is. I've also spoken to the neighbours, but not had any joy there either. In fact none of them seem even to have been aware of our presence.'

'Must have been something extra good on the telly that evening.'

'Don't really see how much farther I can take it.'

'Difficult, I agree, when one doesn't even know what sort of a person one is looking for.'

'Or that such a person exists.' Sergeant Raikes's tone was reproachful.

Manton gazed moodily through the windscreen. 'I'm sure I detected perfume in the room.'

'Passfield's, perhaps. He uses some fancy after-shave lotion.'

'How do you know?'

'Station sergeant told me. Passfield wanted an officer to go out and buy him some after he'd spent a night in our cells.'

'And did anyone?' Manton asked with amused interest.

'He was told that Elizabeth Arden only visited the station on alternate Mondays.'

'Anyway, this was nine o'clock in the evening,' Manton said, with a frown. 'Even the fanciest after-shave lotion wouldn't hang about the face all day.'

'Well, sir, unless you can suggest a further line of enquiry, I don't think there's anything else we can do at the moment.'

'Nor do I—at the moment.'

The Bromleys' house was a modern one-storey building standing, as the house agents would say, secluded in half an acre of attractively landscaped garden.

Rita Bromley was reclining in an expensive undulating chair on the terrace at the back of the house when the officers arrived. She heard the discreetly melodious chime of the front-door bell and hurried into the house to open the door. She was expecting to find her husband's solicitor on the threshold.

'Oh, it's you!' she observed sourly. 'Well, I've got nothing to say so you can go away.'

'We'd like to come in,' Manton said.

'That you're certainly not doing. I know my legal rights and you don't step inside this house without a warrant.'

'We've anticipated your needs and brought one with us.'

Rita Bromley ran the tip of her tongue round her magenta lips. Her hair, which was the colour of pink champagne, was swept up into a pattern of whorls which looked as firm as those you might find in sand after the tide has gone out. She was dressed in a pair of tight mauve slacks and a blouse-cum-shirt which had Chinese dragons climbing all over it.

'What is it you're looking for?' she demanded angrily. 'Whatever it is, you won't find it here.'

'Possibly not,' Manton replied equably, 'but we'll still look.'

It was clear that Rita Bromley didn't intend letting them out of her sight, so turning to Sergeant Raikes, he said, 'You search the bedroom, I'll start in the living-room.' Her look of undiluted hate did his heart good; also the fact that she elected to remain with him seemed to indicate that the living-room was the more likely source of discovery.

'Very nice place you have here,' he remarked as he idly opened and closed the doors of the cocktail cabinet and peered behind a picture on the wall above it. 'Favourite place for safes,' he said by way of explanation. 'But obviously not George's.' He gave her a wry smile. 'Where is his safe, by the way? Surely he has one.'

'Don't expect me to help you,' she said, watching him with eyes which glittered like two pieces of uncut glass.

He had just completed his tour of the room which reminded

him more than anything of a Cary Grant–Audrey Hepburn film set when the telphone started ringing.

'Go ahead and answer it,' he said, as she looked from him to the instrument and back again.

She walked stiffly across the room and lifted the receiver.

'Hello ... oh it's you, Lew ... look I can't talk now, the bloody police are here.... They have a search warrant ... no, I'll call you as soon as they've gone. And that can't be too soon for me,' she remarked as she dropped the receiver back on its cradle and hurried after Manton who was on his way through the door.

'Let's see if we can find George's study,' he said aloud to himself. 'I take it he does have a study?' he added as Rita rejoined his side. She merely glared at him and he called out, 'Where are you, Jim?'

'Still in the bedroom, sir,' Sergeant Raikes answered from a room at the end of the hall.

Manton strolled over to the door. 'Found anything?' he asked quietly, shielding the room from Rita's view.

'Only a lot of very expensive clothes.'

'All hers?'

'Some of his, too. Monogrammed silk shirts and pyjamas you'd never dare go to bed in, and the sort of suits that require a valet's permanent attention.'

Manton closed the door to continue his own examination of the premises with Rita still following him like a tame iceberg.

The kitchen reminded him of an operating theatre in a new chrome and glass hospital. The dining-room came straight from Heal's best window. It was while he was in the dining-room and gazing out of the window that his eye fell on an annexe at the back of the garage.

'What's that used for?' he asked. Rita Bromley merely stared fixedly over his shoulder, however, and he stepped out on to the terrace to go and investigate.

A paved path led round the back of the garage and to the solid oak door of the annexe. He tried the handle and wasn't surprised to find it locked. He turned to Rita who was still his shadow.

'Key, please.' When she showed no sign of responding, he said in a suddenly tough tone, 'The key, Mrs. Bromley, unless

45

you want to find *yourself* in a prison cell as well. I mean that.'

She hesitated a further second then turned on her heel and retraced her steps to the house. This time with roles reversed, Manton followed her. From her handbag which was on the sofa in the lounge, she took out a key and handed it to him.

'Thank you,' he said. 'Now perhaps we shall get somewhere.'

Once more they wound their way round the edge of the garden. Manton opened the door and stepped inside, followed closely by the ubiquitous Rita.

'Quite the home board-room,' he observed drily as he looked around. At one end was an old-fashioned solid mahogany desk, complete with red leather top. On the opposite side of the room was a long table with six chairs set around it. In between the desk and the table was a round coffee-table, with a heavy glass ash tray as its only adornment, and three or four easy chairs with a matching sofa against the farther wall.

Manton walked over to the desk and tried the drawers. To his surprise, the first one opened: less to his surprise, there was nothing in it. He looked across at Rita Bromley who was leaning against the wall by the door in an attitude of watchful insolence. The remaining drawers were similarly all unlocked and empty of anything of significance.

'You seem to have been busy spring-cleaning,' he said, as he began pulling the drawers right out and laying them on the floor.

'Naturally, it's the time of year,' Rita replied with an unmistakable crow of triumph in her tone.

Stooping down, Manton peered into the drawer cavities; then plunging in an arm he extracted a folded brochure.

' "Suntrap Tours",' he read aloud. ' "Choose your own Mediterranean beach and we do the rest".' He glanced up. 'I'm afraid the Riviera will have to manage without George this year. I doubt whether he'll even be able to choose his own cell.' He returned his attention to the brochure. 'But what's this! "Suntrap Tours will not only make all your reservations but can supply you with travellers cheques as well, thereby obviating the weary necessity of the would-be voyager shuttling between travel agent and bank." Now, isn't that interesting,' he remarked, once more looking across at Rita whose expression had become suddenly venomous. He put the brochure into his pocket. 'This has certainly made *my* journey worth-while.' His glance went round the room. 'Where's the safe?'

'Find it!' The words came out like a witch's curse and caused Manton to raise a mocking eyebrow.

'I'll do my best.' After a thoughtful pause which might have conveyed the impression to an intruder that they were engaged upon a parlour game of some sort, he walked over to the sofa and pulled it out from the wall. 'Right first time,' he said in a cheerful tone as the door of a small wall safe came into view. 'Open it, please.'

'Why should I?'

'Because if you don't I shall arrest you for obstructing me in the exercise of my duty.'

'I don't know the combination.'

'And I don't believe you!'

'George changed it recently.'

'Then I'm arresting you.'

'You can't. It's not my fault if I don't know how to open my husband's safe.'

'If it'd been true, you'd have said so in the first place. However, either you open it or I arrest you and then come back and blow it open.'

'George'll kill me.'

'I doubt it. Anyway there's no precedent for a prisoner murdering his wife during a visit.'

'Bastard,' she muttered.

'Cut the compliments and open the safe.'

Shielding it with her body so that he couldn't observe her manipulation of the lock, she quickly and dexterously opened the safe. As she stepped back, Manton knelt down in front of it and began to examine the contents.

If he had hoped to find any travellers cheques he was disappointed, though there was a very considerable sum in cash. He reckoned several thousand pounds in £5 notes. Money apart, there were title deeds to the house, stock certificates relating to investments in three highly reputable companies and a small red address book. Manton seized this eagerly. People did not normally keep their address books locked away in safes unless they were blackmailers or secret agents, or

47

cautious crooks like George Bromley.

To Manton's dismay, however, there appeared to be no more than three or four entries and none of them of immediate interest.

The first fell under 'C' and was *Cullis and Monk, Bournemouth* 584312. The next under 'N' was *Nation and Pilfer, Bristol*. Then came under 'O', *Oxford* 793548 and finally under 'V', an entry which read *Box 546, Hauptpostamt, Vienna,* 1.

Manton copied the details into his pocket-book and was flicking the pages of the address book to see whether he had missed anything when Sergeant Raikes appeared.

'Any luck, sir?' he asked.

'What do you make of this?' Manton tossed him the address book. 'Bearing in mind it was locked away in a safe.'

'Shouldn't be difficult to find out who these various people are. These first two sound like firms of solicitors.' He turned it over several times in his hand as if an examination of its cover might reveal additional secrets. 'Shall I hang on to it, sir?'

'Yes, I think we'll take it even though I have made a note of the contents. The other thing of interest is this.' He pulled the brochure from his pocket and handed it to Sergeant Raikes. 'Read that paragraph one from the end on the third page.'

'So!' Sergeant Raikes said with a thoughtful nod as he returned it to Manton. 'The ice floe begins to shift.'

'Perhaps,' Manton remarked cautiously.

. They had just regained the house when the front-door bell chimed musically and Rita Bromley darted ahead of them into the hall. Voices, sharp and urgent, floated back into the room, and a second or two later she came back in turn followed by a short, rotund man with balding head and an expression of vigorous alertness. Manton recognised him immediately as Morris Woodside, George Bromley's solicitor. They had exchanged a few terse words at court when Manton had decided that he was not exactly a lovable character.

'Mrs. Bromley tells me you have been searching her house and behaving offensively into the bargain,' Woodside said without preliminary. 'I should like to see the search warrant.'

Manton produced it. 'You'll find it's perfectly in order.'

Woodside frowned at the document. 'It's extremely widely drawn.'

'The court granted it.'

The solicitor passed it back. 'Let me make it quite clear, Superintendent, that if I think you've exceeded your authority at any point in this case, I shan't hesitate, on behalf of my client, to issue the necessary writs against the police.'

Manton shrugged and turned to leave. He'd been too long on the job to allow himself to be rattled by aggressive lawyers. After thirty years in the force he was afraid of no one, not even the Commissioner, though that didn't mean that he did not from time to time privately suffer some bad moments.

For instance, he paled at the thought of what could happen if Mr. Woodside was representing Tony Dayne.

CHAPTER EIGHT

ROGER ELWIN signed the last of the day's letters which his secretary, Miss Carne, had brought in a few minutes before and laid on his desk with a meaningful glance at the clock. It was the evening on which Miss Carne and her mother went to the pictures each week, and, to be fair to her, the only one on which she was apt to show restive signs if she thought he had become unaware of the hour. He pressed the bell and she materialised before him as if he had rubbed Aladdin's lamp.

'I've signed my letters, Miss Carne,' he said, as though she were about to accuse him of the contrary. 'I expect you'd like to be away.'

'If there's nothing else, Mr. Elwin....' He shook his head. One day, however, he would summon up the courage and reply. 'As a matter of fact there is, Miss Carne, there are four wills and three draft leases I'd like you to type before you go.' Miss Carne had been with the firm for thirty years and Roger had inherited her from Mr. Rufford, whose private secretary she had been for the greater part of that time. He still felt that she had him on probation and hence the frequent and almost unbearable desire to outrage her sense of stately complacence. The fact remained, however, that she was efficient to a degree of quite frightening omniscience, and Roger didn't ever dare go further than amusing himself secretly at her expense. Like many of the law's hard-working minor servants, she took great pride in her knowledge of its jargon and in particular of its latin tags which she would let drop with a quiet air of self-importance. For her things never began afresh but always *de novo* or *ab initio*. Others, less easy to work into conversation, obtruded like dissonant notes in a symphony, Roger had evolved a system whereby he privately awarded her points for every tag so used, the object being to see whether she could beat her own highest score which stood at the moment at seventeen. This was on a day when she had managed to come forth with *ex abundante cautilla* and *de bene esse* in the course of a single conversation. The whole satisfaction of the game derived, of course, from her blithe unawareness of the sport she provided for her employer.

After Miss Carne had departed, Roger found his mind turning, as it inevitably did these days, to his defence of Tony Dayne. He had hardly begun pondering afresh, however, when the telephone rang and Mr. Woodside's implacable tone came down the line.

'In view of our common interest, I thought I'd better have an early word with you, Mr. Elwin,' he announced briskly. 'I'm sure you'll agree it's important that none of us get out of step in this case. I've spoken to the solicitors defending the other accused and they agreed that I should take the initiative in co-ordinating our efforts.' He didn't wait for any answer but went on, 'I assume you've had an opportunity of taking instructions from your client?' Roger made a sound indicating that he had. 'Then you know the general line to be adopted. My own view is that it might be a lot worse.' Roger forebore to ask how. 'Our respective clients will doubtless recall various further details which will assist their defence,' Mr. Woodside observed in a tone of breathtaking blandness. 'By the way, have you decided what counsel you're going to instruct?'

'No, I'm still considering that.'

'Oh! I'd have thought you'd already have retained somebody,' Mr. Woodside said with a clear note of reproof. He went on to mention the names of the two he was proposing to brief in George Bromley's defence. Roger knew of them as a pair of thoroughly wily practitioners, who had earned themselves reputations in criminal defence work for their fearless frontal assaults on the police. 'This looks like being a dirty case,' Mr. Woodside added with a certain biting relish, 'and one in which we must be prepared for some vicious infighting with the police.'

'You think that?' Roger heard himself asking in a faintly vacuous tone.

'I certainly do. If the police find themselves short of evidence, as they will, they'll be up to all their usual fabricating tricks.'

Roger, who had, on the whole, a healthy respect and admiration for the police and who accepted that they were men of integrity until the contrary was proved, had a natural urge to disclaim any association with such a view but realised that it might be imprudent to do so. Mr. Woodside, no less than his client, was not someone to cross unnecessarily.

'Bromley has instructed me,' Mr. Woodside now went on, 'to leave no stone unturned in finding out who tipped off the police. I imagine your chap is also anxious to know that.'

'He certainly is,' Roger said with fervour, 'though we're unlikely to get very far. As you know, the courts protect officers from disclosing their sources of information.'

'I'm perfectly well aware of that,' Mr. Woodside replied with asperity. 'But there are sometimes ways of finding things out other than by asking a direct question.' After giving time for this to sink in, he said, 'It'll probably be necessary for us all to meet before long. In the meantime, I'll pass on to you anything I glean and you'll doubtless do the same. Fortunately, this isn't a case of a cut-throat defence, and we can concentrate our combined efforts on attacking the police without fear of any internecine strife among our own clients.' At this point Mr. Woodside emitted a mirthless chuckle and, after bidding Roger a brisk good-night, rang off.

Talk about being caught between the devil and the deep blue sea, Roger thought ruefully, and with ice skates on at that. Any sense of being flattered that he had initially experienced when Manton urged him to accept his present role was submerged by a rising tide of resentment. What he was most aware of was that the whole messy problem of Dayne's arrest had been shovelled on to his plate and that there was no one to whom he, in turn, could pass even a slender slice. Manton undoubtedly was feeling the better for having achieved just

51

this; moreover, it was the more delicate half of the problem of which he had divested himself.

Roger rested his head in his hands and groaned aloud. Unique though his situation might be, he presumed that he must proceed on the accepted principles governing a solicitor–client relationship. Stated briefly, these were that the client's interest predominated on every occasion. That was fine where the interest stood out clearly like a poplar tree in an apple orchard. But what exactly was Dayne's interest? According to himself it was not to be subjected to any treatment which would seem to distinguish him from his co-defendants. This meant that he would stand trial with the rest, give lying testimony with the rest and eventually end up in prison serving a lengthy term with them. He made out that he was, if necessary, prepared for all this, though in the same breath that he avowed it, he made it equally plain that he expected something to be done for him. But what? And by whom? The police had already made one attempt to let him go and had their efforts repulsed. Now that he was in custody, the Home Office was presumably the only department which could help him. Roger didn't know how these things worked, but he presumed that there would be no problem in effecting his release even now, if it could be done to Dayne's own satisfaction. Always that *if*. He really was playing impossibly hard to get—or rather to forget! And as if all that was not su^fficient, here, via the undauntable Mr. Woodside, was a further complicating ingredient in the suggestion that the defending solicitors should all pull together. That was just the trouble, Roger mused, he was being pulled in too many directions at the same time. And that wasn't all.

Although Dayne had told him where he believed his interest to lie, Roger still had a duty as his legal adviser to avail his client of any defence the law might offer. And a preliminary consideration of the matter told him that Dayne had an excellent, copper-bottomed defence and one that is rarely open to an accused. It is one of the basic principles of the criminal law that you cannot commit an offence without a guilty mind, or what lawyers and Miss Carne call *mens rea*. And Dayne had no *mens rea*: as far as he had been concerned the whole thing had been a bit of play-acting. He had a complete, legal defence —but one he would certainly shun to use, since it would mean pointing a self-accusatory finger at himself.

Roger shook his head from side to side like some cornered wild animal blindly seeking escape. But he saw none. Sooner or later he would, of course, be able to share, indeed, perhaps, to pass on, his burden of responsibility to counsel, but Manton had asked him to delay this moment as long as possible, and had held out the vague promise that somehow things would have sorted themselves out by then.

He glanced across at the clock on his mantelpiece and saw that it was half past six. He had better hurry since he had promised to pick Carol up at a quarter past seven and must have a meal of sorts before then. They were also intending to go to the cinema.

As likely as not they would meet Miss Carne and her mother coming out.

CHAPTER NINE

THOSE who have never been to prison are sometimes given to wondering to what extent those who are there chafe and fret and conceive stomach ulcers. Naturally there are the chafers and the fretters, just as in a zoo, the lions and tigers accept their captivity with less resignation than, say, the giraffes and ostriches. But on the whole they represent a minority, which is not the same as saying that the majority enjoy being in prison. Merely that they have better resources for dealing with their situation.

George Bromley and his four associates belonged to the majority. However great had been their hopes, or grandiose their plans before events overtook them, a sort of resigned quiescence settled over them once they were inside. Far from surrendering to despair, their minds were actively engaged with the future—a future which would begin on the day they got out of prison whenever that might be.

Whatever the social reformers may say, hope, in fact, is seldom extinguished by even the longest sentence. It may become temporarily dimmed while the judge's words are still ringing in the prisoner's ears but it is unlikely to remain so for long.

Of the five recently lodged in Brixton prison, Passfield fretted the most. Less emotionally stable than the others, he was given to periods of black depression. On the other hand the remainder of them were able to look beyond their immediate plight and to make the required adjustments, which were admittedly the easier for having had to be made before.

Tony Dayne lay stretched full length on his bed, his hands clasped beneath his head. In the cell on one side of him was Bromley, on the other Rutter. He was thankful that he didn't have to share with either of them, or with Armley or Passfield, for that matter. He wasn't aware of talking in his sleep, but he couldn't help feeling that the more you were worried you might, the greater the likelihood that you would.

Like his lawyer, he was trying to think what his best course was. Or to be more exact, whether any variations of the course already discussed might be permissible. He wasn't sure that his solicitor had believed him, but he was genuinely frightened of what would happen to him should any of the others tumble on the truth. What else but a very real fear could have prevented him fleeing when the police were actually eager to look the other way. His expression froze in cold anger as his mind harked back to the bungling mischance which had resulted in his arrest.

His attention was suddenly caught by a sound of metallic scratching somewhere below his left ear. In one neat movement he was off the bed and investigating beneath it where a heating pipe ran through the wall into the next cell. The morter round the pipe had crumbled and a spill of paper now suddenly appeared through a crack. Dayne put out a hand and seized it. As he did so, he became aware of Max Rutter's voice from the adjoining cell.

'Can you hear me, Tony?'

Dayne wriggled further beneath the bed and put his head as close as he could to the crack.

'Yeah, I can hear you, Max.'

'Do you think George can hear us if we talk?'

'He may be able to hear talking, but he won't be able to pick up words unless his ears have turned into radar screens.'

'Good,' Rutter said mysteriously. 'You know that George thinks Freda had something to do with our arrest?'

'Yes.' Dayne's body became tense as the instinct of self-preservation asserted itself.

'Do you, Tony?'

'Do I what?'

'Think Freda grassed?'

'I don't see how she could,' he replied cautiously. 'I told George that.'

'It's you who's convinced him.'

'Me?' Dayne ejaculated.

'Something to do with the way she must have got away. What you told him. Anyway, that's not what I wanted to talk to you about, Tony.' Dayne pressed his ear closer to the crack and waited. 'I think it's much more likely that George himself brought it all about.'

'You mean George grassed?' Dayne asked in surprise.

'No, not exactly that, but that he gave the show away by . . . by . . . well, by being George Bromley.'

'Go on.'

'Hasn't it been clear for some time that he wasn't running things as he was meant to; that he'd become greedy and cagey? He told us less and less and became more and more the arrogant boss. Surely you'd noticed that, Tony?'

'I suppose I had in a way, but I still don't follow how you suggest he was responsible for what happened at the bungalow that night.'

'I believe he had plans to bring in others and was preparing to throw us overboard.'

'He wouldn't have dared.'

'Depends on how he intended setting about it.'

'Well, how?'

'I don't know all the answers, Tony, I'm just kind of thinking aloud. George's wife comes to see him every afternoon.'

'So what?'

'She's always accompanied by that brother of hers, except she came alone to-day.' There was a pause, during which Dayne rubbed his listening ear. Rutter went on, 'I've always thought it funny that George never brought Lew Slater into the game. I'd have thought he'd have preferred him to you or Passfield or even me.'

'Each of *us* was an expert of sorts. I don't suppose Lew Slater knows a travel agent from a strip-tease club. That's why he wasn't in, there was nothing he could do. Anyway, what about Derek, you didn't mention him?'

'No, and you'd better not breathe a word to him of anything I've said. He's right in George's pocket and a vicious young punk at that.'

'O.K., Max, what've you told me all this for?' Dayne asked.

'Obvious, isn't it? Keep your eyes and ears open and your mouth shut where Big George is concerned. If we're not careful, he's going to be running our cases for us. We may have a common interest, but it's not so common that I'm going to have George Bromley dictate my defence to me. And anyway,' Rutter concluded, 'I don't trust him any more. He'll sell us out as soon as pickle an onion.'

A moment later, Rutter had withdrawn from his side of the crack leaving Dayne to wonder whether the older man had been speaking his real mind or had merely been trying to lure him, Dayne, into some indiscretion. If this, it could only mean that they were already suspicious. But how could they be?

Nevertheless, it provided him with additional thinking matter when he resumed his stretched-out position on the bed.

For a second he listened attentively, but no sound at all came from the cell on the other side.

CHAPTER TEN

IT didn't take Manton very long to find out that Messrs. Cullis and Monk of Bournemouth, and Messrs. Nation and Pilfer of Bristol were estate agents and that the Oxford telephone number was that of a firm of the same breed. But there the trail stopped almost before it had begun since each of the firms denied all knowledge of George Bromley, as well as of the other names which Manton hopefully gave them. For whatever purpose Bromley had recorded their particulars in his address book, it was one which seemingly belonged to the future.

As to the Vienna box number, Manton had transmitted an urgent enquiry via Interpol for information.

There was a knock on his door at the same moment that it opened to admit Detective-Sergeant Raikes.

'I've just been talking to the lab, sir, about the travellers cheques.'

'Any joy?'

'They say there are a hundred thousand pounds' worth.'

'We told *them* that,' Manton remarked.

'I know, but this is official scientific confirmation,' Sergeant Raikes said seriously.

'I see! What else?'

'The paper on which the cheques are printed appears to be a continental manufacture.'

'Austrian by any chance?' Manton asked, the Vienna box number uppermost in his mind.

'They can't yet determine the country of origin. I gather they mayn't even be able to do so at all, but they are going to make further tests.'

'Why don't they consult the Bank of England or the Mint?'

'I think they will, though they didn't say so outright.'

'What about Suntrap Tours? Any luck in that direction?'

'That's what I really came to see you about, sir. Suntrap Tours was Bromley and his pals. There's absolutely no doubt of it. The office has been closed since the arrest, and people I've spoken to in the area have given descriptions which fit Dayne and Passfield.'

'What about the others?'

Sergeant Raikes shook his head. 'No, Dayne and Passfield seem to have been the only two anyone saw around.'

'So that's how the forgeries were put into circulation,' Manton said thoughtfully.

'It looks as though Dayne and Passfield bore the brunt of most of the work, which helps to explain why Dayne became disgruntled and decided to grass. He presumably saw the others living it up while he had to go through the motions of working every day.'

'Enough to sour anyone,' Manton observed in a sardonic voice.

'Don't you think it's a possible explanation, sir?'

'Could be.'

Sergeant Raikes looked hurt. He'd been working like a zealous beaver and was not displeased with his deductions, even if his Detective-Superintendent remained unimpressed. Normally he'd have been number 4 in the chain, but both the

Detective Chief Inspector and the Detective-Inspector were away. The one with a fractured ankle as a result of slipping down the front steps of his own home: the other on an advanced course at the police college, whither he had gone ten days ago with considerable diffidence and a massive supply of aspirin. The result was that Sergeant Raikes found himself performing at least two other people's jobs as well as his own. Not that there was anything particularly exceptional about this in police circles where the day on which the full complement in any division or area was on duty belonged to the millennium.

'Any further developments over Dayne, sir?' Raikes asked, thinking to relieve the silence by a change of subject.

'None that I'm aware of,' Manton replied, moodily. 'That particular piece of music still has to be faced, and make no mistake about it, Jim, we're the ones who are going to do the facing. When things go wrong as badly as that did, you needn't think anyone is going to stand up in public for you.'

'I guess our shoulders are broad, sir.'

'It's not my *shoulders* I'm worried about! Do you realise it only needs a breath of what's happened to reach the long ears of one of our less benign M.P.s and before you know where you are there'll be a public enquiry, following which I'll get the sack, Dayne'll get murdered and the most forgotten fact of all will be that we caught a bunch of crooks about to unpack the fattest haul of forged travellers cheques ever found in this country.'

Sergeant Raikes grinned. 'Occupational risks all around us and not a cent of danger money.'

'It's all right for you, you're still young enough to run away to sea,' Manton said, glancing without joy at his sergeant's unperturbed expression.

Raikes continued to grin since he couldn't think of anything to say and it occupied his features. It never dawned on him that his ever-buoyant spirits were apt to jar on those intent on a period of self-immolation. The truth was that he thoroughly enjoyed his work in a healthy, extrovert way and was incapable of understanding, still less sympathising with, his fellow officers who agonised and grumbled their service away. It was Manton's view that he would make a good Flying Squad officer where 'Theirs was not to reason why . . .'

Manton rose from his chair. 'There's only one thing to do,' he declared with sudden new-found vigour. 'And that is start again at the beginning and see what we've missed.'

'Missed?' Sergeant Raikes looked puzzled.

'Yes, missed. Somewhere there must be a clue as to how the forgeries reached the bungalow. Everything points to the fact that they hadn't long been there when we arrived, so we've got to find that clue; and that means going back to the beginning.'

'Yes, sir.' Sergeant Raikes nodded, but without enthusiasm.

CHAPTER ELEVEN

Two days later the five prisoners appeared in court on remand. It was to be a purely formal occasion in the sense that the prosecution was not yet ready to proceed and Manton would merely step into the witness-box and ask for a further week's remand in custody. If the defendants raised no objection, that would be that and the whole thing would be over in a matter of a couple of minutes.

But everyone knew by the time the moment arrived, that the defendants, through their various legal representatives, were going to raise every conceivable objection that a lawyer's ingenuity could devise. Accordingly, there was thunder in the air within, as well as outside, the court.

Roger Elwin arrived determined to play it by ear. Dayne hadn't instructed him to make a fuss, but obviously if all the others were going to, it would be politic to associate himself with the general defence clamour. Moreover, since there was no possibility of inducing the prosecution to open their case, the prospect (dim though it might be) of securing bail was enhanced. Indeed, the longer the police conceded they would require to prepare themselves, the greater the chance that the court would release the defendants on bail. And once Dayne was out on bail, Roger reckoned that he would hear no more of him. It seemed to him, therefore, that this would offer the smoothest and most practical severance of the Gordian knot which was tied so constrictingly round his client's neck. But the whole thing depended, of course, on their all being given

59

bail, not that there seemed any danger of different treatment being meted out to individuals.

Shortly after Roger had taken his seat, Mr. Woodside came in, accompanied by the junior counsel whose name he had given Roger on the telephone.

'I've got counsel here, even though it is only a formal hearing,' he said, leaning over toward Roger. 'It's as well to let everyone see that we mean business. We're going to press for a date to be fixed and also for bail. I take it you'll associate yourself with both applications?'

'Surely.'

'Good. As Bromley's name is first on the charge sheet, it'll be for us to kick off anyway.'

A few minutes later the defendants were brought in and the atmosphere of reunion was complete.

Roger noticed that Dayne was right in the middle with two on either side of him. It seemed somehow symbolic of his plight, almost as if he was under the guard of his own colleagues. Nevertheless, he looked his most sleepily relaxed and gave his solicitor a friendly wink as their eyes met.

Roger thought he detected a look of faint apprehension on the faces of the two lay justices as the prisoners were brought in and their legal advisers faced the bench as though lined up for a bayonet charge.

The jailer, a bull-necked police constable whose tunic resembled a skin he'd outgrown, announced in a sergeant-major's voice, 'Remand number one, sir, George Bromley, Maximilian Rutter, Anthony Dayne, Derek Armley and Roy Cecil Passfield.'

Manton who had been hovering to the rear of the witness-box now stepped forward and said in his most deferential tone, 'I respectfully ask for a further week's remand in this case, your worships.'

'In custody?' asked the clerk.

'Yes, sir.'

The clerk turned a faintly quizzical gaze on the row of lawyers, whose bayonets were now gleaming more brightly than ever. 'You've heard the police application, gentlemen, are any of your clients applying for bail?'

Bromley's counsel was on his feet and charging. 'All of them.' He glanced along the row for support and received it in a series of vigorous nods. 'Though my own application is only for Mr. Bromley.'

'Very well,' the clerk said, 'pray proceed.'

'Before I do so, I should like to ask the superintendent some questions,' counsel said, swinging round to face Manton. 'How long will it be, Superintendent, before your enquiries are complete?'

'I can't say, sir.'

'One week, two weeks, two months, a year? You must have some idea.'

'Definitely less than a year, sir.'

Bromley's counsel glared angrily. 'Is that supposed to be funny, officer?'

'No, sir. I was trying to answer your question.'

'Try again, and this time seriously.'

'I can't say when our enquiries will be complete. We still have many more to make.'

'And while you go about things at your leisure, you're proposing to keep the defendants indefinitely in custody?'

'It's not his decision whether or not they remain in custody,' the clerk broke in.

'And I can assure you that I'm not going about things at my leisure,' Manton added.

'I think,' the clerk said, looking in Manton's direction, 'that their worships would like to know when you will be ready to proceed.'

'I hope to be in a better position to let the court know next week, sir.'

'You may need to be,' the clerk replied suavely. He turned to counsel. 'Anything further you want to ask the officer?'

'Indeed. What are your reasons for opposing bail in this case?'

Manton looked at him in surprise. 'The gravity of the charge, the likelihood of the defendants absconding and the possibility of interference with witnesses.'

'Those three old hardy annuals,' counsel observed scornfully. 'What evidence have you that Mr. Bromley may abscond?'

'No *evidence*, but anyone who deals in forged currency on this scale must inevitably be tempted to leave the country and avoid his trial if given the opportunity.'

61

'*That* is one of the most outrageous statements I have ever heard a police officer make in such circumstances. However, you did answer my question: you have no evidence that he is likely to abscond. And why do you believe he may interfere with witnesses?'

'For the same reason, sir.'

'Which witnesses are you worried about?'

'I'd rather not say, sir.'

'Rather not say!' Counsel's voice took on a freshly scandalised note. 'I suggest you'd rather not say because no such witnesses exist.'

'That's not so, sir.'

'I invite the Court to press this officer to answer my question,' counsel said dramatically.

'I thought he had,' remarked the clerk.

'I mean, by naming the witnesses he's so concerned about.'

'We can't force him to do that.'

'Then I shall invite their worships to draw the inference that no such witnesses exist.' He swung back to Manton. 'Is your informant one of them, by any chance?'

'Informant, sir?' Roger tried not to show the sudden quickening of his interest.

'The person whose information led you to make this arrest?'

'What about ... the person, sir?'

'Are you concerned to protect him?'

'Or her?' added the clerk, and turning to counsel, said, 'I don't think you're on very fruitful ground. Whatever else you may learn from Mr. Manton, I'm sure it won't be the name of his informant, assuming there was one.'

'We'll see,' counsel remarked grimly.

'But not to-day,' the clerk replied in his blandest tone. 'If you have no further questions. . . .' Counsel signified that he hadn't and the clerk said to Manton, 'Just so that we don't have to go all through this four more times, am I right in thinking that you oppose bail in the case of each defendant and for substantially the same reasons?'

'Yes, sir.'

'Right. Now . . .' He nodded at counsel who was grimacing impatiently, as if trying to hitch his nose to his left ear. Roger watched him in fascination.

It was obvious none of them were going to get bail on this

occasion, but if Manton stalled again next week about fixing a date of hearing, things might be different. The court would become rapidly less compliant with each week that passed without any evidence being given, and Roger knew that the police were nowhere near ready. It was a situation he had every intention of exploiting on behalf of his embarrassing client.

Bromley's counsel might have the reputation of being an astute practitioner, but to Roger's way of thinking his performance which now followed was lamentably mismanaged, not that it would have been likely to have achieved its purpose however skilful its execution. But in the first place it went on too long, in the second it revealed counsel to have an inordinate and scarcely-disguised contempt for the two justices he was supposedly hoping to sway by his words, and in the third it was just plainly embarrassing. Bromley was depicted as a man who had every right to expect early canonisation.

When it became Roger's turn to stand up and make his plea, he did so briefly and earnestly, at the same time managing to give the rather hoary old reasons at least a semblance of freshness.

To no one's surprise, however, all the applications were refused and the court room erupted into noisy disorder as defendants, their lawyers, their friends and relations and their accusers struggled out through their various exits.

'I can't think why you opposed bail,' Roger remarked to Manton when they were a safe distance from everyone. 'You could easily have let two or three of them out, including Dayne, and all your problems would have been solved. And mine, too.'

'How could I!' Manton replied with a touch of impatience. 'You know quite well it had to be all or none, and I'm certainly not letting the lot out, even to help you.'

Roger cocked his head in the direction of Mr. Woodside and counsel who were standing talking on the steps of the courthouse. 'They're absolutely determined to find out who shopped them.'

'We're used to that.'

'I suppose there's no question of any of your boys leaking anything.'

Manton looked at him sharply. 'What are you suggesting?'

Roger shrugged. He felt in no mood to placate anyone at the moment. 'Who stands to benefit by my client's removal from the scene?'

Manton's expression turned to one of amazement. 'Are you seriously suggesting that the police might deliberately leak something as a step toward getting Dayne's throat cut?'

'You must be tempted. . . .'

'Good God!' Manton's tone was incredulous. 'I know the public take a certain pleasure these days in believing that we can stoop even lower than a snake's belly, but that anyone could really think we'd do what you've just suggested, well I'm dumbfounded.'

'I'm quite sure you personally wouldn't,' Roger said quickly, taken aback by the depth of Manton's reaction. 'But after all, that sort of thing has been going on in one form or another since Uriah the Hittite was despatched into the forefront of the hottest battle. And I imagine the security service practises the art with a fair amount of gusto. And certainly criminals themselves are not above a bit of treachery if it'll serve their ends, so why *your* sense of outrage at the suggestion that the police might go in for the same thing.' Manton appeared thoughtful and Roger went on, 'That's your trouble, you have to cope with increasingly ruthless and ingenious crimes, but you want to retain your public image of being splendid sportsmen who wouldn't dream of breaking any of the rules of fair play. I don't happen to have acquired my ethics from the public school code-book. I think more starry-eyed, hypocritical nonsense is talked about our so-called incomparable system of justice than about anything else. I suspect a number of other countries have just as good and even better systems than ours. I'm also sure that a good many have a darned sight worse. But for heaven's sake don't be shocked just because I suggest you must be tempted to take an attractive, if immoral, course which might solve the problem of my troublesome client. Remember we're concerned with tough criminals, not innocent maidens.'

'Well, I *am* shocked,' Manton replied emphatically. 'And I hope I always shall be at such a suggestion. And whatever you may say I still think ours is the finest system of justice in the world. You've only got to look at all the countries which have adopted it.'

'Had it imposed on them, you mean.'

Manton snorted. 'Are you going to say that you'd sooner be dealt with in a Russian Court than a British?'

Roger shook his head pityingly. 'No.'

'Or in a French Court in which you're assumed to be guilty until you prove the contrary?'

'It works fairly, I believe, under their particular system of procedure,' Roger retorted. 'You see, I don't happen to accept that we have a monopoly of justice in this country.' His face broke into a sudden grin. 'Anyway, on behalf of my client, I'm delighted to hear the views which you've expressed.'

'Well, come in and cement your delight with a cup of canteen coffee,' Manton said, as they reached the entrance to the police station.

Roger cast a hasty look around him. None of his fellow lawyers appeared to be in sight. 'It's your fault I behave like something out of an early spy film,' he remarked, as he noticed Manton's expression of sardonic amusement.

'Come up to my office,' Manton said as they entered the building, 'and I'll send down for some coffee. It won't taste any better there, but at least we can drink it without an accompanying smell of baked beans on toast.'

'I quite like baked beans,' Roger remarked.

'So do I, but I can do without their reminder when all I want is a cup of coffee.' Manton threw open the door of his office and held out an expansive arm to usher Roger in. He let out a groan as he caught sight of the mound of papers sitting in the middle of his desk. 'That's the real trouble with the police these days. Bumph!'

'You should employ the same tactic as the Duke of Wellington,' Roger replied.

'What was that?'

'Oh, when he was being pestered in the middle of some campaign, he wrote to the War Minister and said words to the effect that if he attempted to answer the mass of futile correspondence which surrounded him, he would be debarred from all serious business of campaigning. I remember he talked about "the futile drivelling of the mere quill-driving in your Lordship's office", which has always struck me as a particularly pleasing descriptive phrase.'

Manton laughed. 'Wish I had the guts to do the same thing.'

'It's not your guts which are lacking: just your rank. You can get away with that sort of thing when you're a commander-in-chief and a duke to boot.'

Manton picked up the 'phone and ordered the coffee at the same time thumbing quickly through the pile of paper. Roger noticed a sudden quickening of his interest as he extracted a single sheet from half-way down the pile and read it intently.

'News from Vienna,' he said, without looking up. 'That box number address we found at Bromley's home belongs to somebody of the name of Fischer.'

'That all?'

'No, it's not,' Manton said in a pensive tone.

'It also says that a girl named Freda Fischer has been found murdered.'

CHAPTER TWELVE

ROGER waited impatiently for Manton to go on but finally broke the silence himself.

'Does it say how Freda Fischer is related to the box number?'

Manton shook his head. 'There's no attempt to connect the two bits of information.' He picked up the 'phone and asked to be put through to Detective-Sergeant Raikes. 'Have you seen this message which has come through from Vienna, Jim?'

'Yes, sir, came in while you were across at court. I didn't know you were back yet.'

'What are we supposed to deduce from it?' Manton asked.

'I imagine they'll tell us more when they have something.'

'Yes, but is the murdered Freda Fischer supposed to have any connection with the box number?'

'Couldn't say, sir,' Sergeant Raikes said in his maddeningly cheerful way. 'Presumably they must think she does, or they wouldn't have bothered to mention it.'

Manton put down the receiver and gave Roger a helpless shrug. 'You heard that?' Roger nodded. 'Suppose we must wait for the next instalment from Vienna. I only hope it's not as cryptic as this.' He held up the report and let it slide through his fingers.

'I imagine Fischer is as common a name in Austria as Fisher is in this country and they didn't want to make any false assumptions. On the other hand they may have been hoping you could help them.'

'How?'

'Since you were enquiring about the box number, you might, for all they knew, have heard of some Fischers in general and of a Freda Fischer in particular.'

'I suppose that's possible,' Manton conceded. 'Meanwhile, it's merely tantalising.'

A police cadet brought in two cups of coffee, and Roger reflected with secret amusement that this vital service had become a traditional part of training in every profession and trade.

The telephone rang and Manton stretched out an automatic hand to answer. His expression became suddenly alert. 'Something further from Vienna,' he hissed at Roger over the top of the mouthpiece.

Roger watched him, making an occasional note as he listened in silence, broken only by the odd monosyllable, to what was coming down the line.

'O.K. I'll call you back, when I've digested what you've just told me. Meanwhile, I take it they'll pass on anything further they discover. . . . Fine. . . . No, I'll definitely 'phone you soon and suggest something.' He replaced the receiver and turning to Roger said, 'The Freda Fischer who's been murdered was in England last week. They found entries in her passport showing she arrived here on the day we made our arrest and left again the next.'

'How was she murdered?'

'Strangled.'

'In Vienna?'

'Her body was apparently found in a small wood on the outskirts of the city about a quarter of a mile from where she lived.'

'Anyone yet been arrested for the crime?'

Manton shook his head. 'So far, I gather, they've very little to go on.' He smiled ruefully. 'Indeed they'd like our help in finding out what she was doing here on such a short visit, as it might turn out to have a bearing on her death.'

'Anything else known about her?' Roger asked.

'Age, twenty-four. Just over one and a half metres tall, weighs fifty-six kilos. Fair hair, blue-grey eyes.'

'Married?'

'Not told.'

'Did she live alone or with somebody?'

Manton shook his head. 'All we've got at the moment is what I've told you.'

'Well, it's a start,' Roger said encouragingly. 'It gives you something to work on.'

Manton gazed at him with a disconcertingly thoughtful expression.

'And you, too.'

'Me?'

'I'd like you to pay another visit to Brixton and find out from Dayne everything you can about Freda Fischer.' He observed the look of dubious caution on the solicitor's face. 'Surely you've no objection to doing that? After all, it may assist your client.'

Roger put down his cup on the edge of Manton's desk with unnecessary care and got up. 'O.K.,' he said slowly, 'but no promises. Remember I'm Dayne's representative, not yours.' He grinned. 'And I can't even be bought with a cup of canteen coffee.' He moved across to the door and, with a hand resting on the knob, added, 'Anyway, I'll certainly go and see him, and if he does tell me anything, I'll then decide how much I can properly pass on to you.'

'I'm not sure that I always like you,' Manton remarked. 'Professionally, that is.'

Roger laughed. 'Oh, I heartily reciprocate *that* sentiment.'

CHAPTER THIRTEEN

IT was the next afternoon that Roger drove to Brixton prison and parking his car in the shadow of its solidly encompassing wall, joined a small throng of people at the main gate who were waiting to be admitted.

He was shown into a different waiting-room on this occasion, though it managed to be just as cheerless as the other.

During the ten minutes he waited for Dayne to appear, he gazed out of the window and tried to imagine what it would feel like to be a prisoner. Being locked up in a cell all day would soon destroy his spirit, but if you were lucky enough to be on one of the numerous working parties which seemed to be endlessly on the move within the prison compound life might be just supportable. His eye fell on one group of three who were carrying buckets and brooms and who appeared to be convulsed in laughter. He would like to have known the cause of their mirth.

The door opened and a prison officer stood aside to let Dayne enter.

'I wasn't expecting you to-day, Mr. Elwin,' he said with a faintly quizzical expression. 'It was only yesterday we saw each other at court. Incidentally, do you think there's a chance of our all getting bail next week?'

'I wouldn't bank on it,' Roger replied.

Dayne looked about the room with distaste and sat down. 'Sorry I can't offer you a cup of tea and a slice of the governor's home-made cake, but what brings you here this afternoon?'

'Does the name Freda Fischer mean anything to you?' Roger asked quite suddenly.

Dayne's reaction was to stare at him as though he had sprouted a second head. It seemed an age before he answered, and when he did so his tone was coated with suspicion.

'It may do. Why?'

'She's been found dead in a wood on the outskirts of Vienna.'

For a second Roger thought Dayne was going to leap across the table between them and seize him by the lapels. Then his hands fell abruptly to his side, and he said in a strangely detached voice, 'Dead, did you say?'

'Strangled.'

'And why are you telling me this?'

'Because I think you can probably tell me something.'

'Even if I can, why should I?'

'It could be in your interest to do so.'

'It isn't.'

'You can't tell.'

'I still say it isn't.'

69

'Was she the girl who brought the cheques to the bungalow?'

'It's the police who've sent you along to question me, isn't it?' Dayne demanded angrily.

'It's certainly the police who told me about Freda Fischer's death, but I'm still your lawyer, not theirs.'

For a time, Dayne stared with bright-eyed concentration at the surface of the table. Eventually he looked up and said, 'I'd sooner you laid off this angle, Mr. Elwin. You must take my word for it that it won't assist my case.'

'I'd prefer to judge that for myself.'

'Just take it from me.'

'And what about the others?'

'What about them?'

'Does her death affect any of them?'

'It doesn't affect the position of any of us.'

'And you decline to tell me what you know about her?'

'Oh, heck!' he said in a tone of sudden weary resignation. 'You've guessed she was the girl who brought the stuff to the bungalow. Apart from that and her name, I don't know anything else about her.'

'Would Bromley?'

'I presume so.'

'And the others?'

'Can't say. Probably no more than me.'

'How many times had she been over?'

'I met her for the first time the night we were arrested,' Dayne replied, looking straight into Roger's eyes.

'You've no idea who murdered her?'

'You joking? I've been locked up in Brixton these past ten days, what am I supposed to know about murders in Vienna?'

'You might have been able to guess,' Roger replied in a briskly matter-of-fact tone.

'Well, I'm afraid I can't.' He paused. 'Anyway, who did kill her?' he asked sharply.

'The Austrian police are still searching for the murderer.'

'Without knowing whom they're looking for?'

'That's what I understand.'

'Honest?'

'Yes, honest, Dayne,' Roger replied coldly.

'Sorry, Mr. Elwin, no offence meant.'

'Though, I don't know why,' Roger went on in the same chilly tone, 'I should be frank with you, when you're the reverse with me.'

Dayne managed to look like a small scolded child.

'But I have told you all I know,' he expostulated.

'Not very willingly.'

'Well, I had to think.' His tone became cajoling. 'You suddenly blow in here with news of this girl's murder. I know you're my lawyer and all that, but I'm in a tight spot and I need to work out my position all the time. It's not that I don't trust you, but there are some things you just have to think out for yourself.' He gave Roger a wry smile. 'But now you know as much about Freda Fischer as I do.'

'O.K.' Roger replied in a neutral voice, making a mental note to follow up the matter further.

'And you're going to leave things there?' Dayne's tone held a note of tentative anxiety.

'I don't seem to have any choice, do I! A solicitor can only act on the instructions he receives from his client.'

'Fine,' Dayne said, with relief, adding blandly, 'thanks for coming along this afternoon.'

Thanks for nothing, Roger felt like saying sourly. If there was one thing he resented it was being led by a ring through his nose by his criminous clients. However, it didn't seem that the interview could be carried any farther. His overriding impression was of Dayne's anxiety lest he might begin probing Freda Fischer's background. His relief when Roger appeared to accept that he should now drop the matter had been almost childishly transparent.

The question was, of course, why had he been so anxious in the first place. The fact that neither Dayne himself nor any of the others had given so much as a hint of Freda Fischer's presence at the bungalow seemed to indicate that they were of a common mind so far as that particular matter was concerned. But if that was so, then a complete new field of speculation was opened up, for once doubt was cast upon Dayne, it followed automatically that the whole perspective was changed and that the role of the others could be different from what it had hitherto seemed. Was it possible that Dayne's own role of informant was all part of their plan? Though heaven knows what the plan could involve.

Dayne's voice brought Roger back to the reality of the drab interview room. 'Shall I see you again before the next hearing, Mr. Elwin?'

'Not unless anything special crops up,' Roger replied, one half of his mind still chasing theories.

'You're going to have another bash at getting me bail, aren't you?'

'I thought you didn't want it, unless the others got it, too.'

'That's right.'

'Because if you did, the police would still be willing not to oppose it.'

'If I get it, it'll have to be despite police opposition. And I imagine Passfield and possibly Rutter might get it at the same time, too, in those circumstances.'

'You still don't want to be singled out for special treatment?'

Dayne shook his head vigorously and drew a finger across his throat, while making a sound like rending calico.

'I'm serious, Mr. Elwin. Bromley wouldn't think twice about expunging me from the scene. And if you think I could just slip away and change my name and grow a beard and live happily ever after, I'm telling you that this particular fairy story would end with murder. So long as there's any risk of their connecting me with what happened, I'm sticking right beside them.' He stared in silence for several seconds through half-closed eyes at the door, then said with quiet intensity, 'If only . . .'

Roger waited but nothing further came. Dayne's expression, however, told its own story. A story of fear and cunning.

CHAPTER FOURTEEN

BY the time Roger returned to his office, Miss Carne was sitting at her desk with the cover of her typewriter on and her handbag placed reproachfully beside it. He noticed that she also had on her going-home shoes.

'Anything happened while I've been out, Miss Carne?' he asked as blithely as he could.

'Detective-Superintendent Manton would like you to call him, Mr. Elwin.'

'That all?'

'I've dated your letters to-morrow as I thought you wouldn't be back in time for them to be posted this evening.'

'That's all right. No one will notice.'

Miss Carne frowned. One would certainly never have heard the late Mr. Rufford giving vent to such irresponsible observations. Why, the outcome of whole weeks of titanic litigation could depend on the date of one letter. Miss Carne sought around for an appropriate latin tag but her mind only came up with *de minimis non curat lex* which expressed the very opposite of what she wanted.

'They can all wait till tomorrow,' she said severely, 'and I'll see that they catch the nine-thirty post in the morning.'

'Good.' Roger felt in no mood to do other than submit to her dictatorship. Indeed, as far as he was concerned, she could post the bloody letters up a chimney. 'Thank you for waiting for me, Miss Carne,' he managed to say as he passed on to his own room, 'but don't hang around any longer. I have one or two things to deal with and I won't forget to 'phone Superintendent Manton.'

'Then I'll say good-night, Mr. Elwin.'

'Good-night, Miss Carne.'

Roger closed the door of his office and sat down. His hand went out to the telephone, but then rested on top of the instrument. He wasn't sure that he wanted to speak to Manton just yet. He wanted to do some thinking first. By the morning he would have decided what he was going to say to him.

He reflected with a degree of pampered satisfaction that it was one of the evenings when he wouldn't have to get his own supper but would find Carol already harnessed to the kitchen stove when he arrived home. Not only would he be fed, but he could lay his problems in her lap as well. She had a good practical mind which, allied to natural feminine intuition, made her someone whose views were worthy of respect.

Running his car straight into the garage, Roger switched off the engine, got out and scampered round to the back door in one continuous movement. He hadn't intended to pause at the door, but was forced to by finding it locked. He rattled the latch and a second later Carol opened it, and he kissed her extra warmly.

'What's this in aid of?' she asked, examining his face with an air of faint surprise.

'Just to show that I love you.'

'You've got something on your mind,' she said suspiciously.

'How do you know?'

'When you kiss me like that, it means either that you've bought me a present or you're going to unbottle a problem. And I don't see any presents.' As she spoke, her eyes searched him as effectively as if she had patted his pockets with her hands.

He smiled ruefully, 'Yes, it's problems not presents, I'm afraid.'

She kissed him lightly on the mouth. 'If you really want to know, I like problems better. They're more flattering.'

After Roger had fixed them a drink, and while Carol was still busy in the kitchen, he told her about his visit to Brixton and of the various doubts which had arisen in his mind as to the course he should now adopt in relation to Dayne's affairs.

'Surely there's only one thing you can do,' Carol said almost as soon as he had finished speaking. 'Go to Vienna.'

Roger looked at her with a mixture of astonishment and pity. 'And who, may I ask, is going to pay for me to go to Vienna?'

It was Carol's turn to look pitying. Here she had given him a clear answer to his problem and all he could do was respond with a paltry quibble about who was to pay.

'Who usually pays on these occasions?' she asked non-chalantly.

'The client.'

'Then let him do so on this.'

'You don't seem to realise that Dayne would sooner pay me to keep away from Vienna.'

'All the more reason for you to go.'

'Look, darling,' he said, patiently. 'Solicitors can't just go careering about Europe in defiance of their client's instructions. It's not done. The Law Society would frown from a great height. And anyway someone has to provide the money.'

'The police then.'

'The police!' Roger exploded. 'I'm not representing the

police. Why on earth should they pay to send me to Vienna?'

Carol sighed and shook her head sadly. 'You really are making difficulties, aren't you?' She lifted a hand. 'Now just listen to me before you start expostulating all over again. Have you not said all along that this is a very unusual case?'

'Agreed.'

'And that you took on Dayne's defence at the special request of the police?'

'Yes.'

'And that because of the very special nature of the case, you've been receiving police co-operation?'

'Ye-es.'

'And that as soon as it can be achieved in an unobtrusive way, Dayne will be let out?'

'Heaven knows when that day will present itself.'

'And now as a result of what Dayne has told you to-day,' Carol went on, 'it is clear that the murder of this girl in Vienna is tied up with your case?'

'It's an inference.'

'Well then, somebody has obviously got to go to Vienna, haven't they? And you're the natural choice.'

'I can only go if I'm instructed,' he said stubbornly. 'And Dayne certainly won't do that. As I've told you he's more than anxious that I shouldn't go probing in that direction.'

'Well then let the police send you. After all, whatever you say about having Dayne's instructions, the fact remains that it was the police who originally asked you to take on the case. It's obvious that part of the truth lies hidden in Vienna and it must be in everyone's interest to have it ascertained.'

'That's where you're right off the rails. It may be against a whole lot of people's interests to have the truth revealed.'

'But not against Dayne's or that of the police.'

'I'm not so sure about Dayne. Anyway, supposing I did go and supposing I uncovered something which reflected badly against Dayne, what should I do then?'

'Supposing your galoshes leaked and you got wet feet and supposing you then caught a cold. . . .'

'No need to be sarcastic,' Roger said tartly.

'But all this supposition when the issue's so clear.'

'I'm quite certain Manton won't think it so clear when I speak to him in the morning.' His face broke into a sudden weary grin. 'Tell you what, let's open another bottle of wine.'

After they had finished their meal and washed up, a domestic chore which Roger appeared rather to enjoy—at any rate he much preferred it to gardening—they sat on the sofa to watch a television drama in which a boy-friend of a cousin of a girl-friend of Carol's was appearing. It was a small part (indeed he died a messy death in the first five minutes) and the play proved to be as gripping as a moribund octopus.

'Shall I switch it off?' Carol asked lazily.

'Only the sound. The light's rather soothing don't you think,' Roger replied.

She returned to the sofa and settled herself comfortably against his side. For several minutes they sat in silence while he quietly stroked one of her ears.

'If I did go to Vienna, would you come with me?' he asked abruptly.

'And who'd pay for me?' she asked.

'Oh, we'd manage it somehow.'

'Who's we? Messrs. Rufford, Rich and Company?'

'Good heavens, no. They wouldn't buy you a cheap-day return to the next station down the line unless they were sure of getting their money back. No, if you came it would have to be privately financed. Perhaps your father . . .'

'Mention money to him and he immediately becomes a bank manager dealing with a customer who wants an overdraft.'

'But that's what banks are for. If they didn't provide overdrafts, they'd be out of business.'

Carol gave a derisive sniff. 'Do you know that he once made me surrender my watch after I had borrowed a pound from him, so that I should understand some dreary banking principle or another?'

'Borrowing against security, I expect.'

'No, it was something much more involved than that.'

'Did you ever get your watch back?' Roger asked with interest.

'I suppose I must have, but I don't remember. I was only twelve at the time.' Carol turned her head and studied his face closely. 'Anyway, what's all this about your going to Vienna?' In a gently hectoring tone, she added, 'Who's going to pay for you all of a sudden?'

'That's still the crux of the matter,' he said firmly, 'and

unless somebody does, I can't go.'

'But you'd like to?' she asked in a coaxing tone.

He was silent for a moment, then said thoughtfully, 'Either I bow out of this case or I undertake a bit of investigation myself. I can't carry on with one arm tied behind my back by the police and one eye bandaged by my client. I now feel quite definite about that and I shall tell Manton so.'

'He won't want you to throw up the case.'

'I imagine not,' Roger agreed. 'Then he must do something to help me. If he won't, I quit.'

*   *   *

The next morning Roger called on Manton on his way to the office.

'May I use your 'phone and tell Miss Carne I'm here?' he asked as soon as he was in Manton's room. 'It'll save her sending out a search party, and my having to endure one of her unspoken reprimands later.'

Manton made an inviting gesture in the direction of his telephone and watched while he made the call.

'I wonder you don't pension off that old trout,' he remarked genially, as Roger replaced the receiver. 'She can't do your business much good.'

'She's an extremely efficient secretary,' Roger replied stoutly.

'She's a tiresome old cow and you know it. However, tell me about your visit to Brixton yesterday afternoon.'

Roger told him, and then went on to report the decision he had reached.

'But you can't back out now,' Manton expostulated. 'Apart from anything else it would be highly unprofessional. You'd have the Law Society on your tail.'

Roger shrugged. 'I doubt it. Anyway, it's up to you.'

'This is plain demanding money with menaces.'

'The police can afford it.'

'But there's no precedent for the police paying someone's expenses in such circumstances.'

'There's no precedent for a good deal of what's happened in this case,' Roger retorted. 'If you put it up to your bosses that it's in the police interest as much as in Dayne's that I should go to Vienna, I'm sure they'll agree.'

'But is it in the police interest?' Manton queried.

'Cross your fingers and hope. You can't expect to have guaranteed results. But my journey, if I do go, should at least help to bring us a little closer to the truth. Whether or not that will prove to be in anyone's interest is quite another thing.'

When he left the police station, Roger felt better. He had reached his decision and delivered an ultimatum, and found himself almost hoping that the answer wouldn't be too soon forthcoming.

CHAPTER FIFTEEN

TWO days later, Manton telephoned Roger just as he was about to leave his office and asked him if he could fly to Vienna the next day. Roger, whose mind was entirely elsewhere at the time, reacted with a stunned silence, but eventually managed to say that he would come over and see Manton straight away.

Miss Carne who had listened in to the conversation on her extension but who knew nothing of any prospective trips to Vienna gave him the oddest look as he passed through her office on his way out. It caused Roger to reflect that should he at that moment drop dead, she would find it difficult to live up to one of her more favoured tags, namely *de mortuis nil nisi bonum*, which she was fond of uttering with a pious flutter of her eyelids after a derogatory reference to one of the firm's deceased clients.

'That was jolly quick,' Roger said when he reached Manton's office. 'I thought it would take weeks to get a decision.'

'A fat lot of use that would have been,' Manton replied. 'I had hoped to have it all fixed yesterday, but the A.C. was away and I couldn't see him until this afternoon.'

'I didn't realise that this was going to be a direct approach affair.' Roger still sounded bemused.

'Apart from three of us at this station, the District Detective Chief Superintendent and the Assistant Commissioner himself, and you, no one knows about the cock-up over Dayne's arrest.' He noticed Roger's expression. 'This isn't a matter we've put in writing and sent coursing round the usual channels. It's being dealt with as though it were a piece of sensitive dynamite, with everyone kept well clear of the site save the bomb-disposal boys.'

'Of whom I am one!'

'You most certainly are. Anyway,' Manton went on briskly, 'persuading the A.C. was easier than I had expected. He accepted that we had a responsibility toward Dayne and that the circumstances required someone to go to Vienna and find out exactly what the situation was there and that you were a suitably neutral person to undertake the mission.'

'I'd call myself neutralised rather than neutral,' Roger remarked.

'Whichever it is, the A.C. thought you were the right person to go, and he's prepared to underwrite your expenses within reason.'

'I don't care for the sound of those last two little words.'

'Nothing to them. All they mean is that you shouldn't take the imperial suite at a deluxe hotel or prolong your stay unduly.'

'And what would be regarded as *unduly*?'

'Well,' Manton said with an expansive air, 'I imagine you'll be able to do everything in three or four days at the outside. Possibly in less.'

'And what exactly are my terms of reference?'

'To find out everything you can about the Fischers of Box number five-forty-six, and whether Freda Fischer's death has any connection with what's happened here.'

'I take it you'll give me a letter of introduction to the Vienna police.'

'Yes, and we'll cable them, saying that you're an emissary.'

'And it's clearly understood that if any conflict of interest arises between you on the one hand and Dayne on the other, I naturally resolve it in favour of my client.'

'I doubt whether any such conflict will arise,' Manton said airily. 'But if it does, you'll doubtless be guided by your conscience.'

'Yes, but my conscience won't be guided by the fact that the police are footing the bill.'

'No, quite,' Manton remarked in an abstracted tone as he gazed out of the window. Bringing his attention back to Roger, he said, 'And you'll be able to leave to-morrow?'

'It doesn't give me much time. . . .'

'Why do you want more? All you have to do is pack your razor and toothbrush and tell your guardian dragon of a secretary that you'll be away for a few days. If you can leave to-morrow, you'll probably be back before the remand hearing next week, and that would be a good thing from both our points of view.'

Roger nodded. 'O.K., if you can get me a seat on an aeroplane, I'll be off to-morrow.' As he spoke he realised that this put paid to any chance of Carol being able to accompany him, not that it had ever been more than slight in the first place. But clearly she wouldn't be able to come at this short notice.

Occupied with his own thoughts, he was only vaguely aware that Manton was busy on the telephone and started when he heard him say, 'Well, that's fixed. You're booked on a B.E.A. flight leaving London Airport at nine-thirty-five. It arrives in Vienna at one-forty-five, which'll give you the afternoon to get down to work.'

'What about a hotel?'

'Walk in to one when you arrive. You won't have any problem at this time of year.'

'And money?'

'The banks will be open before you go.' He grinned. 'Or if you like, I can let you have some travellers cheques at a discount.' Manton suddenly paused. 'Incidentally, you had better take a few with you as samples. The Vienna police might be able to help over their manufacture.' He rose and came round his desk to where Roger was sitting. 'Well, it remains only to wish you a pleasant journey, a successful trip and a safe return. And when you're about to dig into a second of those dreamlike cakes, remember not only your figure, but the taxpayer's pocket.'

'Any more advice?' Roger enquired.

Manton shook his head and looked suddenly serious.

'I just hope you're not going to return empty-handed. At the moment this case is like a corpse with the head missing, and we'll not get any further until the head has been found. And my guess is that it'll be found in Vienna, if it can be found at all. So it's up to you.'

'Head-hunter to the police!' Roger murmured in a sardonic sotto voce, as he made his way out of the station.

He returned to his office and left a short note propped against Miss Carne's typewriter informing her that he'd been called away on sudden business and expected to be back in a few days. He resisted the temptation to end it *Vale*.

When he reached home that evening he telephoned his senior partner who received the news with unquestioning equanimity. The partners of Rufford, Rich and Company were not given to interfering in each other's cases or even to offering one another advice unless it were sought. Mr. Rich knew no more than that his junior partner was defending one Dayne and that this now required him to visit Vienna. He assumed, correctly, that this wouldn't have to be paid for out of petty cash.

Finally, Roger called Carol.

'Did you say *to-morrow*?' she asked with a note of dismay, after he had blurted out the news.

He explained that he had and why there was urgency. He also deemed it tactful to stress the all-work-and-no-play angle and indeed felt little compunction about doing so since this appeared to be the prospect. Matthew, he added, would appreciate some attention in his absence.

He went upstairs to bed feeling tired, excited and, above all, resigned. But if anyone had asked him to what, he could only have replied that it was to the unknown.

CHAPTER SIXTEEN

ROGER'S foreign travel had consisted to date of a couple of weekends in Paris, a wet fortnight spent on the Belgian coast and a three-week tour of Switzerland and Italy, with the Rhineland thrown in on the way back.

He had never been to Austria, and his knowledge of German extended no further than half a dozen strangely pronounced words.

He enjoyed the flight, particularly the last part which provided him and his fellow-passengers with some spectacular mountain scenery off to their right.

Schwechat Airport seemed intimate and welcoming compared with the busier ones of Western Europe and the various formalities were painlessly undergone. He took a taxi into the city and was put down outside the B.E.A. office on the Ring-strasse, the great sweeping boulevard which encircles the old city on three of its sides.

He explained his hotel requirements to a slightly severe-looking young man and was directed, rather as if he had been asking for the nearest strip-tease joint, to a hotel which lay close to the Karlsplatz and was not more than a quarter of a mile away. At least, this was what he reckoned after convert-ing metres uncertainly into yards.

First sight of the hotel was encouraging and, if the interior didn't wholly live up to the smart new façade, it didn't fall far enough short to matter. He was shown up to a room which was permeated with a faint, but not displeasing, smell of musty wood, and had thick heavy madeira-coloured curtains which almost certainly dated back to the days of Emperor Franz-Josef.

On the large box-shaped bed was one of those vast encased eiderdowns which resemble great white omelettes. The bath-room was old-fashioned, but had taps which looked capable of filling a pond in a matter of minutes.

After unpacking and having a wash, Roger decided he was ready to begin. As he handed in his key, the porter gave him a pleasant smile and said, 'Would you like a nice afternoon tour, Mr. Elwin? You can go to the Opera House and afterwards out to Grinzing and up the Kahlenberg mountain and through the beautiful Vienna Woods. It is a very nice tour. I have tickets here.'

'Unfortunately I have a business appointment this after-noon.'

'A pity. Perhaps to-morrow then?'

'Perhaps.' Then in an unintentionally conspiratorial tone, he asked, 'Can you direct me to the headquarters of the police?'

The porter looked immediately anxious. 'It is nothing to do with the hotel? You have not been thieved?'

Roger hastily reassured him that it was business and not the management's shortcomings which had prompted the question.

'You know the Ringstrasse?'

'Yes.'

'It is on the Park Ring opposite the Stadt Park.'

'Which way do I turn when I reach the Opera?'

'When you come to the Opera, you turn right along the Kärntner Ring which becomes the Park Ring.'

'Thanks. I'll be able to find it easily now.'

Having spent the greater part of the morning sitting in confined spaces, Roger found it agreeable to stretch his legs; the more so since the sun was shining and Vienna looked a particularly pleasant city in which to walk. It seemed spacious and stately and yet still throbbing with life. Crowded trams rattled across the intersections and the pavements were thronged. Roger paused outside the Opera to gaze at one of Europe's most famous buildings, and behind it the Hotel Sacher whose renown was almost as great. The Kärntnerstrasse down which he had been walking now narrowed as it crossed the Ring and penetrated the inner city. It looked excitingly alive, and Roger determined to explore it later to its length.

Obediently, however, he now turned right and made his way along the gently curving Ring until he reached police headquarters. Pausing only a moment to assemble his thoughts and feel for his small pocket dictionary, he marched inside.

Speaking very slowly and articulating so that his jaws ached, he explained the purpose of his visit to a sallow young man who wore gold-rimmed spectacles and had long lank hair. When he had finished and had produced Manton's letter of introduction, the young man motioned him to wait and disappeared. He was gone several minutes, and when he reappeared, beckoned Roger to follow him. At the end of a long corridor, he threw open a door and stood aside for Roger to enter.

Sitting at a desk which gave the impression of being inches deep in paper was a thick-set man with a fresh pink complexion and a shock of honey-coloured hair which had begun to turn white around the temples. He rose, and with arm outstretched came across to greet Roger.

'Come, Mr. Elwin,' he said in a deep, resonant voice, giving Roger a painful handshake. 'I am Kirschner. Come, sit.'

'I think you know the reason for my visit, Herr Kirschner,' Roger began when he had sat down and his host had nonchalantly swept a number of documents off his desk on to the floor, apparently to make room for his elbows:

'All this paper,' he muttered, despairingly. 'Is it like this too at Scotland Yard?' Perhaps fortunately he didn't wait for an

answer but went on, 'Ya, you want to know about the death of
Freda Fischer. She was—how do you say——' He put his
hands round his throat and made an alarming grimace.

'Strangled,' Roger supplied.

'Ya, strangled, but not with hands. Strangled with . . .' His
glance darted round the room.

'A ligature,' Roger suggested.

'No. With a . . . a . . . a scarf,' he exploded triumphantly.

Roger forebore to point out that a scarf was a form of ligature. After all, he wasn't here to instruct Herr Kirschner in
English vocabulary.

'Have you found the murderer?' he asked.

'No.' Kirschner looked solemn. 'No, he has . . . poof . . .
vanished.'

'Can you tell me something about Freda Fischer? Where
she lived and who with and things like that?'

'She lived in Grinzing—that is a suburb of Vienna—with
her father. It is a small house in a quiet street. Grübaumgasse
number eight.'

'What does her father do?'

'He does not work any more. He is not old, but he is not
healthy.' He managed to make the unhealthy Herr Fischer
sound as though he was suffering from a particularly disgust-
ing complaint.

'And what did his daughter do?'

'She looked after her father and sometimes helped her
brother run his little Weinstube. Her brother, he is married to
a pretty wife.'

'And none of them have been able to help you over Freda's
death?'

'They have been questioned and questioned but they cannot
help. They have been very shocked.'

'You don't suspect them of trying to conceal anything from
you?'

'But of course! But what? One suspects always until the
criminal is found.'

It occurred to Roger that Kirschner's patience under this
barrage of questions might begin to wear a trifle thin, but he
determined to go until the signs appeared. Meanwhile, though,
it might be prudent to show his appreciation of the help he was
being given.

'I hope you don't object to all these questions?' he said. 'I am very grateful to you for your assistance.'

Herr Kirschner beamed. 'Now I help Scotland Yard and then Scotland Yard will help me, yes?'

Roger swallowed uncomfortably. It was embarrassing to be accepted so firmly as the representative of Scotland Yard. Presumably the vagaries of translation and the international teleprinter service were responsible.

'We believe that Freda Fischer came to England two weeks ago to deliver a consignment of forged travellers cheques,' he said, at the same time producing one of the sample cheques from his pocket.

Herr Kirschner took it, held it up to the light, turned it over, smelt it and finally said, 'I keep?'

'Yes. Don't her family know why she travelled to England?'

'It was for a holiday, they tell us.'

'A very short one,' Roger remarked. 'She only stayed a few hours.'

'She had her luggage stolen when she arrived and became very depressed. So she decided to come home to Vienna.'

'Is this what her father has told you?'

'And her brother and her cousin. They have all told the same thing.'

'If she was carrying forged travellers cheques, where did they come from?'

'You'd like me to say from here? Perhaps it is true, but there is no testimony.'

'Are you satisfied that her family are all that they appear to be?'

Herr Kirschner pursed his lips. 'We make many enquiries. They are a very close family. They do not say much to people. But we shall find out more.' He switched his gaze abruptly to Roger. 'But it is not possible that her family murdered her. They have ... alibis. Ya, they give each other the alibi,' he added, fixing Roger with a quizzical eye.

'But you don't believe their alibis?'

'I believe and I don't believe. I am a policeman,' he replied, leaving Roger wondering how far his slightly enigmatic observations were a product of his mind or were merely due to faulty English.

'Did any of her family have a motive for killing her?'

Herr Kirschner shook his head. 'No motive anywhere. A crime without a motive is like a hunt without the smell.'

'Scent.'

'Ya, the scent.'

'But the motive may have to do with the forged travellers cheques.'

Kirschner picked up the cheque Roger had given him and examined it again.

'Good forgery,' he observed, in a resigned tone.

'Will your experts be able to tell us whether the paper is of Austrian manufacture?'

'Ya, ya, they will tell us.'

'I haven't asked you, but who found Freda Fischer's body?' Roger said suddenly.

'A neighbour.'

'But he is ruled out as a suspect?'

'It was a not a he, it was a she.'

'And you are saying that women don't strangle each other?' Roger remarked with a smile.

'Not in England?' Herr Kirschner queried in a puzzled tone.

'Or in Austria,' Roger said, feeling himself being sucked into a linguistic impasse. In an effort to recover the situation he asked, 'Was the neighbour who found the body a friend of Freda's?'

'She was only a maid of thirteen years.'

Roger looked shocked. 'What a horrible experience for her! I suppose she ran home and told her mother.'

'Ya and her mother went to the house of Herr Fischer to tell him, and he became very ill when he heard.'

A silence ensued in which Herr Kirschner shuffled with the papers on his desk, and Roger wondered how much further he could carry his questioning. At length he said, 'It does seem quite certain that Freda Fischer was mixed up with these forged travellers cheques and that she brought them to England from Vienna. We are hoping that you may be able to find out where they came from.'

'I, too, hope,' Herr Kirschner said in an emphatic tone which seemed to hold out more a promise of effort than of success.

Roger looked at his watch and saw that it was half past four.

'I think I might go out to Grinzing this evening and visit the Fischer café. What's it called?'

'Zum Kastanienbaum; at the chestnut tree. There is one outside the Weinstube.'

'Weinstube zum Kastanienbaum, is that what I look for?'

'Ya, it is near to the middle of Grinzing. It is very pretty and you will like it. It is famous, Grinzing, you have heard of it? It is famous like . . . like Scotland Yard.'

Roger nodded amiably. 'I look forward to going out there.'

'Good, Mr. Elwin. Then we will have a further talk perhaps. You give me your address, yes? And how long you stay in Vienna?' He handed Roger a pencil and a piece of paper. 'Please write it.'

'That's my hotel and I shall be staying about three days,' Roger replied, handing back the piece of paper.

Herr Kirschner shook his head sadly. 'It is too short, but Scotland Yard is busy, too, so you must go home.' He laughed good-naturedly at this arrow of outrageous fortune.

He walked along the corridor with Roger and bade him a punctilious farewell at the entrance to the building. Without being able to put his finger on anything specific, Roger was left with the feeling that benevolent as Herr Kirschner had been, he had by no means told him everything the police knew about the Fischer affair. There was no reason why he should have, and the fact remained that he had not. It was over the forgery aspect of the case that he had been particularly unforthcoming. Doubtless, intensive enquiries were at this moment going on and, if this were so, the police might understandably wish to preserve their own counsel—even from Scotland Yard.

As this thought passed through Roger's mind, it occurred to him how embarrassing it would be if he were suddenly to be unmasked as an impostor. It would be too late then to explain feebly that *he* had never said he belonged to Scotland Yard. He quickened his step as he walked away from the building.

He decided to make his way back to the hotel through the old city and with the spire of St. Stephan's Cathedral as his landmark plunged down one of the narrow streets which led off the Ring.

Immediately he found himself in a world of medieval charm, of small squares with fountains, of courtyards and eighteenth-century gabled houses. Every fifty yards or so he would pause and gaze about with an eye enchanted by what it beheld. In the Franziskanerplatz he spotted a restaurant which he made up his mind to visit before he departed. It looked expensively agreeable, and to blazes both with the taxpayer and his waistline.

When he reached the cathedral he stared up in awe at its soaring spire and its high Gothic roof which seemed to dwarf all the buildings clustered around. It was now after five o'clock and he decided he had better get back to the hotel and prepare himself for an evening in Grinzing. He enjoyed the walk along the Kärntnerstrasse, Vienna's main shopping street, and several times was tempted to enter one of the cafés with its enticing display of delectable cakes and pastries. It was with a greater sense of privation than of virtue that he regained the hotel and retired to his room to have a bath and to change.

As he lay contentedly submerged with only his head above the water-line, he wondered what the evening held in store. The longer he contemplated it, the greater grew his sense of unreality. Here he was, Roger Elwin, about to play the role of private investigator in the city of the Third Man.

Well, at least, there was no prospect of *his* being chased through the sewers to a zither accompaniment.

CHAPTER SEVENTEEN

AFTER a consultation with the hotel porter, Roger decided to go out to Grinzing by tram, even though it would mean making a change on the way. However, with such explicit directions as he was given, he didn't think he could go wrong.

As the second tram trundled and lurched away from the centre of the city, he reflected fondly on this disappearing form of transportation. It reminded him of a mythical scaly monster which was harmless and good-natured, until you actually stood in its path when it would let out a sharp, petulant cry of annoyance.

The conductor directed him to the Weinstube zum Kastanienbaum when he got off. Even in the darkness, its huge chestnut tree provided an unmistakable landmark, and Roger reckoned that its roots must stretch right into the foundations of the building.

Though the door was not locked, he thought at first that the place must be closed as all the lights except one were out and there wasn't a soul to be seen. He was just about to withdraw when a door at the back opened and a woman came through. As she did so, she put out a hand and switched on some lights.

'Guten Abend, mein Herr. Bitte um Verzeihung dass sie uns im Finstern finden. Aber ich war in der Stadt und bin spät zurückgekommen.' She paused and looked enquiringly at Roger, then said, 'You are American?'

'No. English.'

'I am sorry we were dark, but I was late in the town,' she explained with an apologetic smile. 'You would like some wine.'

'Very much.'

'What would you like?'

She had come round into the centre of the room and Roger noticed that she was dressed entirely in black. She was short and had auburn hair and the peaches and cream complexion that frequently goes with it. He guessed that she must be the pretty wife of Freda's brother to whom Herr Kirschner had referred with appreciation.

Roger sat down at the end of a bench seat which she motioned him to.

'What do you recommend?' he asked.

'I will give you something good,' she replied, nodding her head to emphasise her judgment. She returned behind the high counter and came back with a bottle and a glass on a round tray.

'Won't you have a drink with me?' he asked.

'Thank you.' She cast him a frankly interested look before going to fetch herself a glass.

'Where is everyone?' he enquired as she poured the wine.

'I do not understand.' Her tone was sharp.

'It's so empty.'

'Oh, that.' She sounded relieved. 'It is early. Later come many people.'

'Where did you learn to speak such good English?'

She smiled. 'You think I speak good English?'

'But, yes. Have you often been to England?'

She shook her head. 'No. I learn it at the school.'

'That's hard to believe. Do your family speak it as well as you do?'

'My family?' She frowned. 'I do not understand.'

'I see that you're married,' Roger said, eyeing the plain gold ring on her left hand. 'Does your husband know England?'

She shook her head briskly. 'My husband is busy man here.' Her tone was unmistakably less friendly than it had been and Roger decided to strike a less inquisitive note.

'It's very nice here in Grinzing. One would never guess that one was on the edge of a large city. It's so quiet and peaceful.'

'It is your first visit to Vienna?' she asked, ignoring his pleasantry.

'Yes, it is.'

He heard an outside door slam somewhere at the rear of the establishment, and a few seconds later a man came through into the room where they were sitting. He paused in the doorway and the woman said something to him in German. Roger caught the word *Englisch*, but that was all. The man replied and then came over to the table where they were sitting.

'It is my husband,' the woman said. 'He does not speak English.'

Roger rose and held out his hand. 'Ich bin Roger Elwin,' he announced with a grin. Turning to the woman, he added, 'And that exhausts my German.'

'Fischer ist der Name,' the man said unsmilingly.

'Did he say your name was Fischer?' Roger looked toward the woman for confirmation and she nodded. 'It is also a good English name.'

There was a silence, in the course of which Fischer went behind the counter and drank a glass of water. When he returned to the table Roger had decided that he would have to introduce Freda's name into the conversation if he was to learn any more. He realised, however, that it might be like crossing two live wires just to see what would happen.

Addressing Frau Fischer he said, 'Funny your name being Fischer. Shortly before I left England, there was a bit in the newspaper about a girl named Freda Fischer being murdered here in Vienna.'

To make the untruth sound more plausible, he went on, 'She'd apparently been in England herself only a few days before her death, which is why it was reported in our newspapers.'

The two faces opposite him had become expressionless masks as he spoke. When he had finished the woman said something rapidly to her husband who shrugged his shoulders and, with his eyes firmly fixed on Roger, made a lengthy reply. Roger had the feeling that part of the exercise had been to test his knowledge of German. Well, they needn't have troubled, there was no simulation about his incomprehension of that.

'She was the sister of my husband,' Frau Fischer now said in a curiously detached voice.

Roger assumed a horrified expression. 'How appalling! I'm terribly sorry ... I hope they've found the person who did it.'

'No, they have not found him.'

'That must make it so much worse. Do the police know who did it?'

She shook her head. 'It is a mystery to all.'

'Where did it happen?'

'Close to here in a wood.'

Roger bit his lip and tried to look suitably shocked. 'And this happened only just after she had returned from England?' he asked.

'Yes.'

'How long had she been in my country?'

Frau Fischer blinked away what might have been tears and said, 'She had her gepäck stolen when she arrived. It made her very sad and she came home immediately. She did not stay at all.'

Roger clucked sympathetically. 'What an awful tragedy! And to think that if she had not had her bag stolen, she might still be alive. How long was she proposing to stay in England?'

'It was just a little holiday.'

'Had she ever been before?'

Frau Fischer consulted her husband before answering. 'Once or twice perhaps. She liked England very well. She had friends.'

Roger tried not to make his voice sound as interested as he suddenly felt.

'I wonder if they lived anywhere near me? My home is just outside London.'

91

'I cannot remember their address, but it was near London, too.'

'Do you know their home?' he asked innocently.

Once more she turned to her husband. 'No, we cannot remember it. It was not an easy name for us,' she added in a perfunctory tone.

He found himself once more up against a stone wall, and he was uncomfortably aware that the man had been studying him with unwavering interest throughout the conversation. However, he now turned and said something to his wife, who nodded.

'What did the English papers write?' she asked, obviously at his prompting.

Roger thought rapidly. They couldn't possibly know whether he was speaking the truth in whatever he now chose to tell them. They already accepted that something had appeared in the English newspapers about Freda's death when this wasn't so. Now was his chance to push home this particular advantage.

'There must have been some sort of muddle over identity because they suggested that the girl found dead in Vienna might have known something about some forged money the police had recently found in a house near London.' He gave an apologetic shrug. 'Obviously it can have had nothing to do with your unfortunate sister-in-law. The muddle probably arose through her bag being stolen. The wires must have become crossed somewhere.'

'Was sagt er?' the man asked fiercely, but his wife shook her head in a gesture of impatience.

'Please tell again,' she said urgently to Roger. 'I do not understand all.'

'I'm so sorry, I hope I haven't worried you. I was only trying to explain that the story in the newspapers must have been mistaken, since they linked Miss Fischer's name with a case involving the discovery of some forged cheques.' He smiled wanly. 'Perhaps they thought her stolen luggage was in some way connected with the other matter.'

The man listened in stony silence as his wife translated this to him. At the end, he said, 'Welche englische Zeitung?'

Minimal as Roger's knowledge of German was, he understood the question and felt his heart miss a beat.

'Which English paper?' The woman asked a second later.

He pretended to think hard, then shaking his head slowly said, 'I can't be certain. It may have been the *Daily Mail*. If not, I think it was one of the evening papers. But I'm really not sure. I could probably find out for you when I return to England.'

Husband and wife held a further colloquy. Then turning back to Roger, Frau Fischer said, 'Please tell more about the forged cheques.'

To Roger, her tone seemed to convey a note of hidden menace. There was more than a polite request for information, and he found himself hoping that some of the Weinstube zum Kastanienbaum's evening customers would start arriving. Fischer's gaze was once more focused on him with disconcerting intensity, and Roger wondered whether he had given himself away. He realised, perhaps too late, that he had shown a certain lack of subtlety in his approach, though he couldn't really see that he would have learnt as much as he had by exhibiting a greater measure of that quality. What he now knew for sure was that the man and woman sitting opposite him were well aware of Freda Fischer's role as a courier of forged travellers cheques. His immediate sense of gratification was, however, offset by the dawning realisation of the peril in which his knowledge had placed him. A peril which seemed uncomfortably near as his eyes flicked round the deserted room and came back to rest on the two watchful faces across the table.

'I can only tell you what I read in the papers and that wasn't very much,' he said with an apologetic smile. 'It just said that three or four men had been arrested for having forged travellers cheques in their possession. I don't recall anything else, I'm afraid.'

'How many men?' Frau Fischer asked, prompted by her husband. 'You say three or four?'

'It may have been more, I just don't remember.'

'And these men are all in prison?'

'As far as I know.' He gave what he hoped sounded like a light laugh. 'I don't imagine the police would want to see them out on bail.'

'Bail? What is bail?'

'The opposite of being held in custody.'

93

'You are a lawyer?' she asked in a suspicious tone.

'As a matter of fact I am,' he replied, cursing himself for having needlessly increased their suspicion of him. The man was now looking at him in a distinctly appraising fashion.

'Do you know names of the men in prison?'

Roger shook his head. 'I'm afraid not. It wasn't a matter I had any particular interest in; just a news item which happened to catch my eye.'

However unsubtle his own approach had been, it was nothing compared with the questions which were now being asked of him. Their very bluntness seemed to indicate an almost frightening degree of self-assurance. But at least they afforded him the opportunity of being similarly direct.

'May I ask why you're so interested in the matter?' He accompanied the question with a friendly and enquiring smile.

'Because of what you say about Freda's name . . .' the woman replied immediately, throwing Roger a challenging glance.

'That was obviously a mistake, as I said.'

Frau Fischer gave a scornful shrug. 'So of course we wish to know what they write about Freda and these men. It is not nice for us to have the sister of my husband mentioned with criminals. Perhaps we must consult lawyer. . . .'

She had made her point, and at the same time succeeded in turning the tables on Roger. Her reply had been so rational as to have made his question sound unnaturally significant.

To Roger's considerable relief, the door now opened and three men entered. They called a cheery greeting to the Fischers and looked at Roger with mild interest.

Fischer went across to them and Roger caught the word 'Engländer'. At all events this was clearly his cue line for departure. He rose and holding out his hand to Frau Fischer said: 'Auf wiedersehen.'

'Good-bye, Herr . . . Elvin? Ja?'

'Elwin.'

He repeated his farewell to Fischer, who merely gave him a curt nod.

On leaving the Weinstube, Roger walked in the direction of the tram stop. He had a shrewd idea they'd be watching him and he wanted them to think that he was about to return to the city. Luckily, the actual halt was just out of sight of the

Fischers' establishment and he walked past it, then ducked down a side road and paused beneath a street lamp to study his map of the city. He saw that Grünbaumgasse was about a quarter of a mile away and that he could reach it without going past the Weinstube zum Kastanienbaum. It appeared to be a short road which petered out in a wood at its farther end.

He had no difficulty in finding it nor in identifying number eight, which was the one from last house on the right-hand side. It was a small, one-storey Tyrolean-style dwelling. Two large trees, in what appeared to be a heavily overgrown patch of garden, completely framed it with their branches, some of which touched across the steep gabled roof like performers in a square dance. The window on the right of the front door was shuttered, but a thin streak of light shone out at one side. Apart from this, the house appeared to be in darkness.

Roger tiptoed up the path and was about to peer through the crack from which the light was coming when he heard footsteps approaching along the road. His line of retreat was already cut off and his only hope was to hide. And the only place to hide was in the shadow of the stout trunk of the tree to the right of the house. He had barely dodged behind it, when the footsteps turned in at the path and a few seconds later he heard a knock on the door. Although it opened and shut almost in one movement, he had no difficulty in recognising Frau Fischer of the Weinstube zum Kastanienbaum before she stepped inside and all became darkness again.

For a while he remained half-leaning against the tree, wondering what he should do next. Finally, he decided to find out whether there was anything to be seen through the crack in the shutters. If there wasn't, he'd go and catch a tram home. Most likely he'd have to do the same, even if there was. In this somewhat uncertain frame of mind he crept forward till he was against the side of the house, where by standing on tiptoe his eyes just reached the lowest level of the window. The shutter which covered it was not properly aligned owing, as far as Roger could see, to a weakened hinge. The result was a narrow, wedge-shaped gap between it and the frame of the window about twelve tantalising inches above his gaze.

There was only one thing for it and that was to find something on which to stand. Picking his way with the utmost care so as not to alert anyone to his presence he set off to explore

95

the garden at the back of the house. Apart from a tiny patch of coarse grass, it consisted entirely of wild saplings and one or two tree stumps which gave it the appearance of a badly-shaved face. Close to the patch of grass was an old wooden chair with the back missing which presumably now served the purpose of a chopping block or shoe-cleaning stand. Roger tested it cautiously and was relieved to discover that at least its legs appeared to be sound. It seemed unlikely that anyone would be needing it at this hour of night and he picked it up and carried it back to the window. Then, after making sure that it was not going to topple over as soon as he climbed on to it, he clambered up and, holding his breath, peered through the crack.

Frau Fischer was sitting with her back to him at the side of a vast wood-burning stove which was adorned with porcelain tiles. The colour motif was blue and white and reminded him of the lavatory fixture in his grandmother's house.

On the other side of the stove was a man of about sixty. At least he certainly looked all of that, though Roger realised it might be the worn face of a younger man. He had a straggly moustache, sunken cheeks and wisps of hair seemed to be falling over his forehead and his ears. On the bridge of his narrow, bony-looking nose rested a pair of steel-rimmed spectacles.

If he was Freda's father, and Roger didn't doubt that he was, he looked as far removed from anything to do with international forgery as a man could. Roger was reminded of Herr Kirschner's comment that her father was *not healthy*. He looked positively seedy as well.

The woman appeared to be doing most of the talking, with the man listening for the greater part in silence. A silence broken only by his constant sniffs which Roger could observe, if not actually hear.

His gaze left the couple beside the stove to take in the rest of the room. Against the far wall was a large oak dresser which stretched to within a few inches of the ceiling. Its shelves were lined with innumerable items of blue and white crockery and at floor level it had two capacious cupboards. In the centre of the room was a round table covered by what looked like a shawl with a fringe all the way round. Behind the old man's head hung the only picture which Roger could see. It appeared to be an ancient sepia photograph of some pastoral scene and, moreover, to be entirely in keeping with its surroundings.

The old man was now leaning forward with the palms of his hands resting on his knees. His expression was of someone beset by difficulties which he had never expected to encounter. He was still sniffing with the regularity of a metronome, and once or twice he slowly shook his head in apparent bewildered disbelief of what his ears were telling him.

At one point, Frau Fischer suddenly swung round in her chair and stared at the window. Roger withdrew his head so rapidly that he almost fell backwards off the chair, but, to his relief, nothing further happened and she turned back again without even getting up.

There seemed, however, no point in remaining on his precarious perch and he stepped down and took the chair back to where he had found it. It was only when he was returning stealthily along the side of the house that the significance of the window's curious height dawned on him. It must mean that there was a basement. A walk round the complete outside of the house confirmed this impression, though if such did exist it didn't appear to have any windows or direct access to the garden.

He gave a shrug. So what if it did have a cellar! A great many houses had them. It presumably also had a spacious attic under that vaulted roof. As he quietly removed himself from the scene, he wondered whether the old man went out much in the daytime. He'd like to have a look round the inside of the house if that could be managed without breaking too many sections of the Austrian penal code.

He had gone about fifty yards when suddenly there was a sound of running behind him and a voice called out, 'Herr Roth, Herr Roth.'

His immediate inclination was to break into a run himself and put as much distance as he could between him and his pursuer. On the other hand, there was something urgently appealing about the voice which made him halt and look back. A girl, her cheeks flushed and her neatly braided hair starting to fall out of place, drew level with him. As she did, her hand flew to her mouth and her cheeks became even more scarlet. 'Entschuldigung bitte! Ich dachte sie wären Herr Roth.'

Roger smiled at her dismay. 'I'm afraid I don't understand.'

'You speak English?' the girl exclaimed in surprise.

'I am English,' he replied.

'I thought you were our neighbour Herr Roth. I am very sorry.'

'There's no need to be. Do you live in this street?'

'Yes.' She pointed at the house next to the Fischers.

'I thought Herr Fischer lived in that one,' he said artlessly.

'No, Herr Fischer lives in the next one. Then this one we live in and Herr Roth lives in the nearest one.' As she spoke her finger pointed eagerly in the direction of the various houses. 'Do you know Herr Fischer?'

'Not well,' Roger said vaguely, and cursed himself for having mentioned the name. 'Do you?'

The girl made a face. 'He does not like children.'

'Are you going to post that letter?' he asked, looking at one she was holding in her hand.

'Yes. Herr Roth goes often to the post-box,' she volunteered, 'and he posts my letters, too.'

'I see. That's why you ran after me. Anyway, I'm sure I can post letters just as well as Herr Roth.' He held out his hand and the girl handed it to him. 'You speak very good English,' he added.

'It is my favourite subject at school.'

'Have you ever been to England?'

She shook her head. 'But I want to.'

'I expect you will one day.'

'Perhaps this summer,' she said eagerly. 'Some will go from my school. If I pass my tests, I shall be allowed to go, too.'

'I'll keep my fingers crossed for you,' Roger said, suiting the gesture to his words.

'Oh, thank you,' she exclaimed happily, as though he'd performed the necessary miracle.

'What's your name?'

'Theo Wächter. Theo is short for Theodora. Do you have that name in England too?'

'Yes, but it's not a very common one. I like it though.'

She pouted doubtfully. 'It is old ... old-customed, do you say?'

'Old-fashioned.'

'Yes, old-fashioned. I would like to be called Tina.'

'Why Tina?'

'It is a nice name,' she replied simply. She looked around

her and then said, 'My mother doesn't like me going out alone any more.'

Roger felt his interest perceptibly quicken. 'Why not?' he asked.

'Not since Fräulein Fischer was murdered,' she replied in a matter-of-fact tone.

'Did you know Fräulein Fischer?'

'Yes. She was nice.' She looked up at him gravely. 'I found her.'

'You mean when she was dead?' Roger asked in a brittle tone.

She nodded. 'I ran all the way home.'

'I'm not surprised. It must have been a terrible shock.'

'You know about Fräulein Fischer? She was your friend?'

Roger thought hard for several seconds. Here was an opportunity not to be missed: on the other hand it was one which required extremely diplomatic handling. One false move and he might find himself in hideous trouble, though luckily he seemed to have gained the child's confidence and there was every chance of her responding willingly to his quest for information.

'Would you mind if I asked you some questions about Fräulein Fischer?'

'What questions?'

'I have come specially from England to find out about her death,' he said in a confidential tone.

'She visited England soon before she died.'

'I know.'

'You are a police?'

'Sort of. Look, Theo, I believe you can help me, but first you must promise not to tell anyone that we have met. It must be our secret.' She studied his face gravely and he went on, 'It is very important that Herr Fischer and his family do not know that we have been talking. Will you promise?'

For a long while she remained silent, and Roger dared scarcely breathe for fear he should disturb her thoughts. At one point she frowned hard and he wondered if she was about to reprove him brusquely and run home even faster than she had originally pursued him. He realised that if rational thinking dictated her answer, that would be the end of his hopes, which lay in the candid trust that only the young or the very simple are capable of according complete strangers.

'I promise,' she said, nodding her head to emphasise the bond.

'I appreciate your trust in me, Theo, and I promise not to let you down.' He fixed her with a solemn look. 'First I want to ask you this, have you any idea who murdered Freda Fischer?'

'No,' I cannot tell.' She accompanied this ambiguous statement by a vigorous shake of the head which succeeded in finally dislodging one of her plaits.

'You don't mean that you know but don't wish to tell me?'

'No, I do not know.' Roger was still unsure whether they were on common ground, but decided to continue and play it by ear. 'Do you think it may have been one of her family?'

The child frowned. 'It could not be, her family loved her.'

'What do people in the street think?'

'Herr und Fräulein Fischer lived alone. They did not talk to many people. Fräulein Fischer cared for her father.'

'Tell me what you did when you found her lying on the ground. Did you touch her?'

'No, no,' the girl shuddered at such a thought.

'How did you know she was dead?'

'Her face . . .'

'Yes, of course,' Roger said hurriedly. 'How did you happen to see her?'

'She was on the ground near the path through the wood.'

'Where does the path go?'

'It is the short way from our houses to the tram halt.'

'Did you see anyone else about as you were coming through the wood?' It occurred to him that the police must already have asked her all these questions, though Herr Kirschner had not seen fit to supply him with such detail.

'There was a man. He was running down the path toward the tram halt. He almost pushed me over, he was so hurried. It was after he had run past me that I found Fräulein Fischer.'

'Did you recognise the man?'

'No, but he went so quickly I could not hardly see his face.'

'But you would have recognised him if you had ever seen him before.'

'I am not sure.'

'Did you tell the police about the man?'

'Yes, and I tell also Fräulein Fischer's brother.'

'He is the proprietor of the Weinstube zum Kastanien-baum?'

'Yes, that is her brother.'

'When did you tell him?'

'So soon afterwards. My mother went to tell Herr Fischer and then Herr Ernst Fischer came to talk to me.'

'How long afterwards was this?'

'Quite shortly.'

'What did he say?'

'He didn't say. He left also quickly.'

'This was before the police arrived?'

'But yes.' Theo managed to convey the impression that the man-in-the-moon could have visited and returned home again before the police arrived.

'What have the Fischers said to anyone since Fräulein Fischer's death?'

'Said to anyone?' she repeated in a puzzled tone.

'What I mean is, have they talked to anyone about it?'

'No. I tell you already they are quiet people. They do not talk to everyone.'

'Do you know why Fräulein Fischer went to England?'

'For her holiday, she tell me.'

'She told you that herself?'

'Yes.'

'Did you see her to talk to after she came back?'

'One time. She had her bag stolen and came home at once. It was very sad for her.'

'Did she have any boy-friends that you know of?'

'She had no time. She was always caring for her father.' Theo's voice carried a note of disgust at the iniquity of this situation.

'So it could not have been a boy-friend who killed her?'

'I do not think. Unless it was a secret friend.'

'Surely there must be rumours going around about why she was killed?'

'Rumours? I do not understand.'

'People must be talking about it. For instance, what do your mother and father think? What does Herr Roth say?'

'We believe it was a mad person. That he meant to do something horrible, but he ran away when he heard me coming.'

Roger pondered this for a second or two. It struck him as extremely unlikely that the murderer would have run in the very direction of the footsteps which were supposed to have put him to flight. It seemed far more probable that he hadn't heard Theo's approach, hence their near collision on the narrow path. And if he had not heard her coming, then she wasn't responsible for disturbing him.

'What time was this, Theo?'

'It was half past eight. Fräulein Fischer had been on the tram from the city which arrives then.'

It occurred to Roger that Herr Kirschner had not told him anything of Freda Fischer's last few hours.

'I wonder,' he mused aloud, 'whether anyone else got off the tram at the same halt.'

'Many people,' Theo replied in at one which immediately killed that line of thought. 'The tram-person-who-gives-the-tickets cannot remember them all, there were so many.' Roger was wondering how she had acquired this particular piece of information when she added, 'His daughter is in my school. She has told us.'

An extension of a previous thought suddenly came into his mind and he asked, 'Do you know whether any of the Fischer family went to the body before the police arrived?'

'Naturally. The police do not arrive so soon I tell you.'

Lowering his voice to a conspiratorial whisper, Roger asked, 'Is there any time of the day when Herr Fischer leaves his house and it is empty?'

The girl searched his face with solemn eyes, 'You are a robber?' she asked.

'No, a lawyer.'

'My father says that lawyers are robbers,' she replied with a wisp of a smile. 'But perhaps not English lawyers. Herr Fischer has his dinner now at the Weinstube zum Kastanienbaum. He goes there at twelve o'clock and stays one hour.'

'That's just what I wanted to know. Incidentally, what does he do all day?'

'He has a work place beneath the house.'

'What does he work at?'

'I think he is engineer,' she replied vaguely. 'He ... he reparates things.'

'Repairs?'

'Yes. I never can remember that word.' She smiled at her own failing.

'I wish I could speak German half as well as you speak English.'

'You do not know any words?'

'Guten Morgen.'

'But it is night,' she exclaimed with a delighted laugh.

'Gute Nacht.'

'Good. What else do you know.'

'Danke schön and bitte sehr.'

'Everyone knows those words. What else?'

'Lufthafen,' he said proudly after searching his brain.

'Ah yes, the airport. You came to Vienna by aeroplane?'

'Yes, in a luftwagen.'

She gave a scream of laughter. 'Ein Flugzeug, not a luftwagen. That is no word, it is translated an air-car.'

'Well, that's exactly what an aeroplane is,' Roger replied in good-natured self-defence. Theo looked down the road in the direction of her house. Interpreting her expression, he said, 'You must go or your mother will wonder where you are.'

'It is still all right. I have not been longer than if I go to the post-office.'

'You have been very helpful, Theo, and I am most grateful. Now, you promise not to say a word to anyone, not even to the police.'

'I have promise.'

He hesitated a moment, then said, 'Let me give you my name and address, and if you come to England, you must get in touch with me.'

He realised that he was running a risk, but the girl had been so forthcoming and trusting that it would have been mean not to have done so. Holding out his hand he said, 'Good-bye, Theo. I expect we shall meet again.'

'In England, yes?'

'I hope so.'

She was still studying the card he had given her when he began to walk away. Her voice called him back.

'Mr. Elwin, Herr Fischer leaves open a window at the back of his house.'

Before he had grasped the full significance of what she said, she had turned and was running like an Olympic athlete toward her home.

Two hours later, when he climbed into bed, Roger found it difficult to realise that this was still his first night in Vienna. He had the feeling of having already been there several weeks.

CHAPTER EIGHTEEN

THE flush of success which had sent him to sleep the previous night had evaporated by the time he awoke the next morning. Reality was no longer in a rose-tinted frame but loomed as harsh as a jagged rock. And as if to emphasise this point he cut himself shaving and was forced to dress while holding a handkerchief to his chin.

After he had breakfasted in the hotel coffee-shop, he went out for a walk, which he hoped might help to settle his mind. It was a bright sunny day with large white clouds bowling across the blue sky under the lash of a biting north-east wind which acquired its cutting edge from the Carpathian Mountains.

He crossed the Ring and strode purposefully round the perimeter of the Hofburg, the old Imperial palace. It was too cold to pause and he did no more than turn his head like a mechanical doll without slackening his pace. Then with all the eager purposefulness of a terrier on to a good scent he shot off down the Ring until he reached the parliament building whose exterior he examined with the same non-stop intensity.

It was while he was striding furiously on toward the town hall that he quite suddenly made up his mind to return to the hotel and telephone Manton. Let the police, who'd put him on the spot in the first place, accept their obligation and give him some advice. Advice as to the extent he would be justified on their behalf in breaking an Austrian law or two.

His cheeks which had become numb with cold while he was out began to feel as if they'd been sand-papered as he sat on the edge of his bed waiting for the call to be put through.

When the connection was made, he was agreeably surprised to find how clear Manton sounded. He'd been all prepared for a frustrating exchange of bellows.

'Well, what have you found out?' Manton enquired immediately.

Roger told him of his meeting with Herr Kirschner, and of his visit to Grinzing.

'The thing is,' he concluded, 'that I think I ought to have a look inside the Fischer's house.'

'I agree. I think you should.'

'Even though it means breaking in?'

'Why not?'

'That's all very well for you a thousand miles away.'

'But you've just said that you think you should.'

'I know, but supposing I get arrested?'

'Send for the British Consul.'

'Forget the British Consul! I want to know what you'll do to help me if anything goes wrong.'

'What can we do? You can hardly expect the Commissioner to write an official letter to his opposite number in Vienna saying that you were acting on his instructions and therefore please give you a pat on the back and send you home.'

'Well, I'm not risking it then.'

'Look,' Manton said earnestly, 'the risks are very small and I'm sure that Kirschner would be perfectly understanding if you did get caught.'

'How do you know? He might be extremely displeased.'

'Unlikely. Anyway, you can't come home with the job only half done.' Manton's tone assumed a further tone of persuasion. 'You've made a good start and, frankly, made much more progress than I ever expected. Admittedly a look round the house mayn't take us any further: on the other hand we can't afford not to know. Why, you might actually come across the presses on which the forgeries are made. Do that and you'll have the police forces of two countries competing to pin medals on you.' Then thinking perhaps that he had gone a little far, he added in a different tone, 'But the decision must be yours and what I've said can't appear on the record.' There was a short silence on the line and Manton went on, 'I'm told that George Bromley became unusually preoccupied after his wife's visit to him yesterday afternoon.'

'Well?'

'I thought you might be interested.'

'Were you?'

'Yes. It seems to indicate that something's happened.'

'You don't think they've found out already about me.'

'I was wondering. I don't see how they could have, but perhaps you had better keep your eyes and ears open.'

'His preoccupation mayn't have had anything to do with the case on the other hand.'

'Don't you believe it,' Manton replied, cheerfully. 'If Big George has a fresh worry, it arises from the matter in hand.'

'What about my chap? Any reports on him?'

'Nothing. You'd better come back before he starts asking for you.' In a dry, deceptively gentle tone he added, 'But complete your assignment first.'

*   *   *

Though telling himself that his mind was still not finally made up and there was plenty of time to withdraw, Roger sallied forth from the hotel once more and directed his footsteps toward Grinzing.

If Herr Fischer left his house at noon each day, it meant that he must be there in time to see him do so, otherwise he wouldn't know whether or not the old man was still inside. The trouble was, however, that Grünbaumgasse was such a quiet, unused street that any stranger hanging about would quickly attract attention. The only thing to do would be to remain in the cover of the wood, close to where the street dwindled into a footpath, and from where he would be able to watch the entrance of number eight. On the other hand, to be caught loitering in a wood, particularly on a day capable of daunting even a Nepalese Sherpa, was likely to arouse even greater suspicion. He had no way of knowing how extensively the short-cut to the tram halt was used, and his final decision would have to be made in the light of events. That is, if he didn't decide to scrap the whole idea.

It was half past eleven when he arrived in Grinzing, alighting at the halt before the one close to the Weinstube zum Kastanienbaum and cutting up through the wood to the Grünbaumgasse. The path must have been about a quarter of a mile in length, and Roger was surprised that anyone, above all any

114

lone woman, should use it at all at night. He could only think that Austrians either had stauncher hearts or less vicious criminals than the English.

Only two other people had got off the tram at the same halt and they walked back down the way from which it had come. He met no one as he walked through the wood and reached the point where the path merged with the street without event.

The Fischers' house was thirty yards up on the left-hand side, and apart from a woman with a small boy walking toward the main road at the far end, the Grünbaumgasse was deserted. In daylight, Roger could see it for what it was, a short, unmade-up road of about a dozen houses, which had been driven into the wood like a narrow wedge.

Roger stepped clear of the path and took up a position behind a tree five yards to the left. He could still see number eight and at the same time was unlikely to be noticed by anyone using the path. He shivered with cold, having left his overcoat at the hotel. If he was going to break into houses, he certainly didn't want the encumbrance of a coat flapping around his legs.

It seemed that he had stood there hours before anything happened. Then almost on the dot of noon, he saw a figure come down the garden path of number eight and turn into the street. Though heavily muffled against the cold, Herr Fischer was still recognisable. He was taller than Roger would have guessed from his sight of him through the crack in the shutter, and he walked with a slight stoop. His hands were deep in the pockets of his overcoat, which appeared to fall almost to his ankles, but what struck Roger most about him was his vigorous stride. There was certainly nothing *unhealthy* about that.

Waiting until he had reached the top of the road and had turned out of sight, Roger left his hiding-place and walked purposefully up to number eight. Equally purposefully he marched up to the front door and rang the bell. What on earth he would have done if someone had answered, he couldn't have said. But fortunately, and not unexpectedly, no one did.

With the merest glance to make sure there wasn't anyone in sight, he slipped round to the back of the house, where sure enough, just as Theo had said, a window was open. He reckoned that it would take him no more than half a minute to open it further and climb in. Before irrevocably committing

107

himself, however, he took a final look around to satisfy himself that he wasn't under observation from the rear of the two neighbouring houses, one of which was Theo's home. This appeared deserted, and the only sign of life from the other was some wisps of smoke coming out of the chimney. Now he was ready.

As he swung his legs round and dropped lightly to the floor, there was an unearthly screech and an indignant cat streaked from beneath his feet. So that was why the window was left open. He thought Theo might have told him. A second later, with a look of intense loathing, the cat had sprung on to the sill and out through the window. It clearly had no intention of remaining in the house with a burglar.

The inner door of the kitchen in which Roger found himself was closed, but he knew it must lead into the hall, which fed all the rooms of the house. This much of the lay-out was apparent from the outside.

In all there were five doors, counting that through which he had just come. The one on the left must be the sitting-room. He opened it stealthily and peered inside. It looked more cluttered than it had through his spy-hole of the previous night and there was a harsh smell of tobacco which seemed almost as anxious to make its escape as had the cat.

Withdrawing quickly and shutting the smell back in, his glance flicked over the remaining three doors. The one over in the corner at the back of the hall was different from the others and resembled more a cupboard door—or, as Roger saw it, the sort which protects a flight of stairs leading to a basement. He stepped across and tried it. It was locked, and securely so from the utter lack of give to his pull. On closer inspection he saw that it was fitted with a small, extremely competent-looking lock which would clearly exercise the ingenuity of a far greater expert than himself. Whoever had had it put there, had not wanted intruders on the far side of the door.

Though Roger's curiosity was now fully aroused, there seemed nothing further he could do to satisfy it. He knew from his previous inspection that there were no outside entrances into the basement.

Frustrated, he turned his attention to the last two doors which were side by side and opposite that of the living-room. He had already guessed that they were bedrooms, and this was soon confirmed. The front one was clearly the old man's and bore the same pungent smell of stale tobacco, even if a trifle less powerfully than the living-room. It was as simply furnished as a monk's cell, and it required no more than a glance to see that it held nothing of significant interest so far as Roger was concerned.

There remained only what had obviously been Freda's bedroom. Indeed at first sight it might still have been so. Her dressing-gown hung on a hook behind the door, and the backs of several pairs of shoes peeped out from beneath a wardrobe. On the dressing-table were a large powder puff, some perfume and a bottle of hair-spray. A framed photograph on a bedside table caught his eye and he picked it up. It was of a woman, taken many years earlier, who he assumed to be Freda's mother. Tucked into a corner of the fame was a small snapshot whose edges had begun to curl. Roger gazed at it hard for several seconds, then removed it and put it in his pocket.

With a final look round the room, he returned to the hall. It suddenly occurred to him that he had not yet come across the bathroom. Surely that wasn't down in the basement! But a further quick reconnoitre disclosed it to be an adjunct of the kitchen, approached through a door which he had earlier assumed to be that of a cupboard.

Before departing, he again approached the locked door and gave it what he considered a rather professional examination. That is, he ran his hands lightly round its edges and over its surface, occasionally giving it small discreet knocks, rather like a doctor palpating a patient with abdominal pains. By the end he was left in no doubt that though it looked the same as the other doors, apart from size, it was in fact a great deal more solid. He gave it a shake but realised he might have been trying to shift one of the doors of Fort Knox.

Wasting no more time, he climbed nimbly back out of the kitchen window, returned it to its original position and darted for the cover of the nearest tree. He decided it would be best to retire via the wood at the end of the patch of garden rather than risk being seen in the street.

If the old man's habits were as Theo had told him, he still had plenty of time before he came back from his lunch. Rather to his surprise he found that it was only ten minutes since he had broken into the house, though while he had been nosing around every minute had seemed like an hour.

Using his sense of direction he steered himself toward the footpath, and stepped out on to it after first making sure that no one was coming.

He caught a tram back into the city after only a short wait and wondered, as it swished its way through the streets, what his next move should be. His mid-day escapade had given him food for considerable thought, some of which he had not yet fully digested.

Arriving back at the hotel, he asked for his key with the idea of a contemplative session on his back.

'A message for you, Herr Elwin,' the porter said, handing him a piece of folded paper with the key.

Roger's look of surprise remained while he opened it. The message was brief to the point of being terse, and read: 'Telephone Herr Kirschner at once.'

CHAPTER NINETEEN

UP in his bedroom, Roger put through a call to the number which Kirschner had given him when they had met the previous day.

'Ach, it is you, Herr Elwin.' He had apparently recognised the voice before Roger could get beyond saying 'Herr Kirschner' in an enquiring tone. 'I must see you at once. Where are you?'

'At the hotel.'

'Stay and I come.'

'What's happened?' Roger asked anxiously.

'Many things. I tell you soon.'

'It sounds very urgent, can't you give me an idea what it's all about?'

'Soon, soon. I am leaving now. If you will wait for me near the door, you will see my car arrive. Come to it and we can drive without stopping.'

'Where to?'

'I see you in ten minutes,' Kirschner said firmly, ignoring Roger's question and ringing off before he could ask any others.

As he made his way back downstairs again, Roger racked his mind as to what could have happened to warrant so much urgency. If he hadn't so recently returned from Grinzing, he would have assumed it was something to do with the Fischers. Well, it still might be, though this seemed unlikely. It certainly couldn't be that the house in Grünbaumgasse had blown up with the old man inside, nor did it seem any more probable that there had been some dramatic turn of events at the Weinstube zum Kastanienbaum. So what had happened?

Cold though it was, he went outside and stood on the step of the hotel and was staring in the opposite direction when a small Porsche braked to a sudden halt, at the same time as a brisk summoning note was sounded on its horn and the passenger door was thrown open. Roger hurried across and got in.

'Good,' Herr Kirschner said in a commending tone as he vigorously engaged a gear and the car shot away from the kerb to internal sounds of protest.

'Where are we going?'

'To Grinzing. You have been there yet?'·

Roger looked at him suspiciously. 'Yes, I went yesterday evening. If you recall, I told you I was going to.'

'Of course, of course. It is very nice there, yes? Perhaps you will have time later to visit the Kahlenberg and drive through the Vienna Woods. It is not the best month, but they are still very nice.'

'But you haven't picked me up merely to extol the beauties of the Vienna countryside?' Roger remarked.

'No, you are right,' Kirschner replied cheerfully. One thing at any rate was clear, whatever was the cause of all the urgency and mystery, it seemed to have whetted his spirits. 'I hope you can help me.'

'How?'

'I want to show you something.'

'All right, but what?' Roger asked with increasing impatience.

'A body.'

Roger's jaw dropped and Kirschner went on in an amused tone. 'You do not ask some more questions?'

'Whose body?'

'Ya, that is the question, whose body?' Kirschner repeated

111

keenly. He gave Roger a sidelong glance. 'Perhaps you will be able to tell me. I hope,' he added, like a small fervent prayer.

'Where did you find this body?'

'I did not find it. A dog found it in a wood at Grinzing.'

'The woods at Grinzing seem full of bodies these days,' Roger remarked.

'They are big woods,' Kirschner replied seriously. 'This body was buried but not very well. The ground is still hard from the winter frost and it is not easy to dig up a big hole.'

'Was it near where Freda Fischer was found?'

'I think you ask that soon,' he said in an approving tone. 'Not near, not far.'

'So there could be a connection?'

'I would not be asking you to come and see this new body if I did not think there was a connection, my friend.'

'Is it the body of a man or of a woman?'

'A man.' His tone seemed to imply that the question was a silly one. He went on. 'He had been . . . how do you say?' Herr Kirschner removed a hand from the steering-wheel and went through the emotions of pummelling his face.

'Beaten up?'

'No, not beaten. After death he had been . . .'

'Mutilated?'

'Perhaps.' He sounded doubtful, however.

'You mean his features had been damaged?'

'Ya. His face is not nice any more.'

'Is it still recognisable?'

'That you will tell me soon.'

'Were there any identifying marks on the clothing?'

'The clothes were English, but that is all. The man had no wallet, no diary, no letters. They had been taken away.'

'How do you know?'

'It must be. No one walks about without something to say who he is. Is not so?'

'Normally, yes. But this man may have removed his own identifying clues.'

'Then he would also have taken the labels off his shirt and his under-shirt and his . . . his under-trousers. Not so?'

'I agree that would be more likely,' Roger replied in a not wholly convinced tone.

'It is logic,' Kirschner said, bending forward to urge the car past a tram before it disgorged its passengers in his path.

It seemed to Roger wholly improbable that he would recognise the body Herr Kirschner was intent on showing him. He could think of no reason why he should be able to. Perhaps, however, Herr Kirschner imagined that those connected with Scotland Yard were in a position to give a name to the corpse of a fellow-countryman wherever it might be found, provided it had come to a sufficiently sticky end.

Shortly after they had passed the turning to the Weinstube zum Kastanienbaum, the car turned left and then right and came to a halt in a narrow, cobbled street directly outside a small, white-washed building.

Roger climbed out and followed Kirschner down a passage which ran at one side of the building. He rapped hard on the door at the end and it was almost immediately opened by a young police officer in uniform, who saluted and stood back when he saw who was his visitor.

The room in which they found themselves was tiled and as cool as a catacomb. Kirschner led the way across to a wooden coffin which was resting on the floor. Bending down he lifted the lid and nodded to Roger to look.

At first, Roger thought he was going to be sick. It wasn't the actual sight, though heaven knows that was gruesome enough, but a sense of revulsion and horror at the indignity of un-natural death. Then making a conscious effort to master his feelings, he stared down at the body, aware of Herr Kirschner's own eager gaze on *him*.

'You recognise him?'

And therein lay a quite unsuspected difficulty. He wasn't sure whether he did or not. It certainly wasn't the face of anyone he knew and yet there was something vaguely familiar about it.

'How long has he been dead?' he asked, continuing to stare at the upturned, contused and lacerated face.

'Five or six days, maybe. He was blown on the back of the head. His skull was cracked.'

'And these injuries to his face occurred after death?'

'During or after death. We have not found the instrument. But you know him, yes?'

'I am not sure,' Roger said apologetically. 'I'm trying to

think whether I have seen his face before and if so, where. The two hang together of course.'

'But you do know him?' Kirschner urged.

'If I don't, I know someone like him,' Roger said in a slow, thoughtful tone. Though he continued to stare at the face, his mind was probing like a terrier's nose trying to pick up a scent. Suddenly he looked up. 'I remember now where I believe I've seen him. It was in court when the forgery gang made their first appearance. I'm almost sure that's where it was.' He glanced down again as if to seek for confirmation of the fact.

Herr Kirschner, meanwhile, looked sceptical. He didn't understand this Englishman from Scotland Yard, who was clearly up to some private game which he couldn't follow. Were the English always so oblique, he wondered. He, himself, was a straightforward policeman and he found life much easier when those with whom he had to deal were the same. But he must persevere.

'Who is the man?' he asked, with a slight edge to his tone. 'You have seen him before?'

'Yes, I'm almost sure that's who he is. It's that chewed-looking ear,' Roger murmured to himself. Looking up he said, 'I can't tell you his name, but he is a relative of one of the men charged with forgery.'

'So! Which is the man?'

'George Bromley. He's the boss of the gang.'

'And this is his relative?'

'Yes. I believe it's his brother-in-law. I don't know him, I've never spoken to him, but I saw him at court with a woman, and Superintendent Manton told me who they were. The woman was Bromley's wife, this man's sister.'

'And now he is dead in Vienna,' Kirschner said in a thoughtful tone. He looked up and, with a gleam in his eye, went on. 'What does Scotland Yard think about that?'

'We now have definite proof of a link between the arrested men in England and the Fischers in Grinzing.'

Kirschner nodded. 'Sometimes,' he said, 'two murders are easier to solve than one. Let us hope it is so in this case.'

CHAPTER TWENTY

DURING most of the journey back into the city Kirschner was uncommunicative behind a rather dirge-like hum which betokened his preoccupation with recent developments. Roger assumed that he would now pull the Fischer family in for further questioning, but he would like to know that this was the intention, as on it depended the length of his own stay in Vienna. The trouble was a conflict of priorities. Roger wanted the forgery aspect to receive first attention, but Herr Kirschner, not unnaturally, was more interested in solving two murders than in scouring his city for the centre of operations of forged travellers cheques. Particularly since they were not apparently in circulation in their home market—always assuming that Vienna was the seat of manufacture.

There seemed to be only one way of finding out what Herr Kirschner was proposing to do next and that was to ask him.

'What's your next move?' Roger enquired in an interested tone, once they had beaten off the challenge of a swaying tram which had threatened to manoeuvre them to a perilous halt.

'An interrogation of the Fischers. You agree?'

'Yes, I certainly do. Will you search their homes?'

'I think it is important, but we must see. It depends on the interrogation.'

'I am told,' Roger said in a careful tone, 'that there is a locked basement in the home of Herr Fischer senior. It would be interesting to know what goes on in it.'

'Who told you that?' Kirschner asked in a voice which was suddenly formal and distant.

'A man I was talking to in the Weinstube last night. I can't tell you his name.'

'And this man spoke English?'

'A certain amount.'

'And you asked him questions about the Fischers?'

'In a discreet sort of way, yes,' Roger answered uncomfortably.

'And what did this man think took place in Herr Fischer's cellar?'

'He had no idea.' Hastily Roger added, 'Indeed, I didn't ask him.'

'You were too discreet, yes?' Herr Kirschner enquired sardonically. 'But now you think that your forged cheques are made in this cellar?'

'It could be so.' Roger felt himself on the defensive under the quizzical nature of the questions.

Rather to his surprise, Kirschner nodded and said, 'Yes, I have not told you that I have received a report on the cheque you gave me yesterday. It came just before I picked you up this afternoon. Our good Herr Doktor Peller says that the paper is of Austrian fabrication, which confirms what Scotland Yard already believes. Not so?'

'Yes. Superintendent Manton will probably wish to call evidence to that effect.' Roger had almost said 'we' before recalling that Manton and he were not strictly on the same side.

Herr Kirschner began to hum again and didn't say anything further until they reached the Ring. 'You like Vienna?' he asked suddenly, with an affectionate glance at the Burgtheater.

'Very much, what I've seen of it.'

'How much longer you stay?'

'I think I'll probably fly home tomorrow.'

'You have already discovered everything?'

'Thanks to your help,' Roger replied smoothly, 'I have learnt as much as I had hoped.'

'Scotland Yard is pleased, that is good.'

'You will keep us in touch with future developments, won't you?'

'Naturally, and you us.'

'Of course.'

'That is how police must work. Always there must be co-operation.'

'Do you think I ought to stay longer?' Roger asked in a slightly worried tone. It occurred to him that Kirschner was being altogether a bit too bland. Although he had spoken about a further interrogation of the Fischers, there was no indication as to when this was going to take place. Indeed, there appeared to be a complete lack of any sense of urgency.

Herr Kirschner hitched one shoulder in a shrug. 'I cannot give dictation to Scotland Yard.'

'If you thought early developments were likely with the Fischers, I could stay another day.'

'I shall have discussion when I reach headquarters. All will depend on that.'

'Could you telephone me after a decision has been reached?'

Kirschner pursed his lips. 'I trust you, my friend, but you know it is not always easy between governments. They pretend to trust but they are suspicious. If I tell you something, it could be bad for me later. You understand?'

'Of course, and I certainly wouldn't want you to think that I am prying into matters which are confidential, but if you can give me an idea whether or not it might be useful for me to stay a further day, I should be very grateful.'

'I will telephone you and leave you message. O.K.?' Herr Kirschner's expression brightened with the settling of this delicate issue, though Roger still regarded it as being in an unsatisfactory state. But perhaps this was because he knew less than nothing about Austrian police procedure.

As the car drew up outside his hotel, Herr Kirschner leant across to open the door for him, and then in an almost continuous movement shook his hand warmly and pushed him out on to the pavement.

'Auf wiedersehen, Herr Elwin. You find for me the name of the man who is dead, yes? I would like to know soon. You go telephone Scotland Yard at once, yes?'

It had already occurred to Roger that further communication with Manton was now necessary, and he went up to his bedroom to put through a call. There was a twenty-minute delay and then Manton's voice came down the line.

'Your calls alone are going to put sixpence on to the standard rate of income tax. What's happened? You haven't been arrested, I hope?'

Roger told him all that had happened since their earlier conversation. At the end, Manton said thoughtfully, 'That's very interesting. Very interesting indeed. I suppose there's no doubt that it is Lew Slater.'

'If that's the name of Bromley's brother-in-law you pointed out to me.'

'No, that's him all right. I'll have to go and see Rita and see how much she knows; or rather how much she'll tell me. This could account for Big George's new worry that I mentioned

117

this morning.' In a cheerful tone he added, 'Well, Lew Slater's no loss to the community and it was thoughtful of him to get done in elsewhere. Saves us a lot of trouble.' After a brief pause, he went on again. 'Why hasn't Kirschner beaten down that cellar door? I'd like to know what goes on there. As it is we shall probably have to call evidence from Vienna.'

'Herr Kirschner may be ready to doff his hat to Scotland Yard,' Roger said tartly, 'but that doesn't mean to say he's at your beck and call. He's conducting this investigation his own way.'

'All right, I get the point,' Manton said with a sigh. 'In that event you'd better come back.'

'I'm going to wait till I hear from Kirschner about Fischer developments.'

'O.K., but you could still probably catch the night 'plane if there is one.'

'I can't.'

'Why not?'

'Because I'm going to the opera to-night,' Roger replied and rang off. Up to the moment of speaking, he had formulated no plans for the evening, but since this looked like being his last in Vienna and he considered he'd earned a night out, a visit to the opera seemed the most obvious of all the 'musts' in the city of Beethoven, Haydn and Schubert.

In the event he saw a performance of Verdi's *Otello*, which succeeded in casting such a spell over him that for three hours he had no thought for anything outside of what went on in orchestra pit and on stage. It was only the third opera he had ever heard, but it ravished his senses, exalted his spirit and left him determined to seize every opportunity that came his way to hear more.

As he walked back to the hotel in this mood of spiritual satisfaction, he reflected pleasurably on Carol's intelligent musical taste. How fortunate that he was going to marry some-one who'd be able to share his new-found joy, which would enrich their life together.

His mind was still far from the matters which had brought him to Vienna when he arrived at the hotel and was handed another of Herr Kirschner's messages with his key.

This one read: 'Don't stay, please.'

The longer Roger pondered it, the more ambiguous its

meaning seemed to become. There was nothing for it, he'd have to call Herr Kirschner in the morning. He couldn't just pack his bag and depart on the basis of this courteous but oddly expressed injunction.

CHAPTER TWENTY-ONE

IT had been while Roger was at the opera that Manton and Detective-Sergeant Raikes had driven over to see Rita Bromley.

Once more they had stood on the doorstep and heard the discreet chime within when Manton pressed the door-bell. Sergeant Raikes had just returned to his superintendent's side and said, 'There's someone at home, there's a light on at the back,' when the door was opened and Rita appeared. She was wearing a pair of black tapered trousers and a flame-coloured blouse, and her hair was this time a slightly lighter shade than the blouse.

'May we come in?' Manton enquired.

'Not unless you have a search warrant.'

'We haven't this time, but it'd still be easier to talk inside.'

'What makes you think I want to talk to you at all?'

'Let's say common interest.'

'Such as?'

'Your brother.'

Rita's expression became suddenly wary and her glance flicked from one officer to the other. 'What about him?'

'I'd like to get in touch with him, where is he?'

'You mean his address?'

Manton shook his head. 'No, he's not there, as you undoubtedly know. Where is he?'

'He's away for a few days, on a business trip.'

'Where?'

'I don't know,' she replied contemptuously. 'He didn't tell me.'

'Abroad perhaps?'

She looked at Manton sharply. 'I've told you I don't know.'

'Vienna, was it?'

The colour drained from her face, leaving her looking suddenly ten years older.

'Do you think we might come in after all,' Manton said agreeably, 'now that we've satisfied you as to the common interest?'

She stood aside and closed the door after they'd entered, then led the way into the living-room.

'What do you wish to know about my brother?' she asked, seating herself as far away from Manton and Raikes as the room permitted.

'Just what he went to Vienna for.'

She bit her lip. 'How do you know he did go there?'

Manton shook his head wearily. 'It's obvious I do know, isn't it? Now let's take it from there and not have so many silly questions.'

'I've told you, he went on business.'

'What business?'

'I don't know. He has a number of interests he doesn't talk much about.'

'I can believe that,' Manton remarked drily. 'Was this particular interest connected with someone called Fischer?'

'I don't know.'

'Did he go there as George's emissary?'

'I don't know.'

'Did he go there to commit murder?'

Manton noticed that she had suddenly begun to tremble, and that her hands were gripping the arms of her chair in an obvious attempt to steady herself.

'I don't know what you're talking about,' she said in a voice which had a frightened rasp.

'Let's have the truth, Rita, it'll make it easier for you in the end.'

'Liar. You're just trying to trap me.'

'Haven't I said enough to show you that I know a great deal more?'

'If you know everything, why come here asking me questions?'

'To exchange information.'

'You've not told me anything I didn't already know.'

'So you did know Lew was in Vienna?'

'You've told me I did,' she replied defensively.

120

Manton ignored the remark. 'When are you expecting him back?'

'He didn't say.'

'Have you heard from him?'

'I'm not telling you.'

'I believe,' Manton went on thoughtfully, 'that you were expecting him back well before now and that you and George are both worried about what's happened to him. That's right, isn't it?'

'Go away and whistle, it'll do you more good than staying here, and I shan't have to listen.' Her tone was a sneer, and made Manton, who was a normally compassionate man, look forward with ugly relish to the approaching moment when he would quietly inform her of Lew Slater's death. There was something about her so predatory, so arrogantly brazen that caused his cruder primeval instincts to come bursting to the fore.

'I suppose you think,' he said in a deliberately unpleasant voice, 'that you would have heard if anything had befallen your precious Lew. That he'd have cabled, that the British Consul would have sent word, even that the newspapers would have contained some item of news if anything like that had happened?' He observed with satisfaction that she was now giving him a sort of wary attention. 'Of course it never occurred to you that he might be up against people of greater cunning than himself. That's the trouble with you and George and Lew, you think you can compete with the really big boys in villainy. You don't know your limitations, though heaven knows you should after this little lot. George inside for the next few years and Lew . . .' His voice trailed away, then he added, 'But of course you don't want to hear from me what's happened to Lew.'

She passed her tongue across her lips and said in a whisper, 'What has happened to him, you bastard?'

'He's dead.'

For several seconds she stared at him in disbelief. 'You're lying,' she said, though without apparent conviction.

'Murdered,' Manton went on.

Her jaw dropped and she gaped at him with a stupid expression.

'How do I know if you're telling the truth?' she managed to say at last.

'What little intelligence you have will answer you that.'

'How do you know this?'

'I've received a report from Vienna. There was a problem over identification, but it was Lew all right.'

'Who killed him?'

'Can't you guess?'

She didn't answer but stared vacantly at the floor.

'Don't you think you'd now better tell me the circumstances in which he went to Vienna?' Manton urged.

'I must speak to George first.'

'Shall I tell you what I believe? George might like to know this too. I think Lew went to Vienna to kill a girl named Freda Fischer, that he did so, but before he could get away he was in turn murdered by one or other of her family.' He paused and went on, 'And if George wants to know what I think the motive was, tell him I know quite well what it was. He believed the Fischer girl was responsible for shopping him and his seedy band of travel agents and he despatched Lew to obtain revenge.' Manton rose, and leaving Rita still gazing numbly at the carpet walked over to the door. 'As soon as I have further news from the Austrian police, I'll get in touch with you.' .

He walked across the hall and opened the front door as Detective-Sergeant Raikes hurried after him.

'O.K. to leave her alone in the house, do you think, sir?'

'Why not?'

'You don't think she'll do anything silly?'

'Such as?'

'Take her life.'

'What? Rita Bromley commit suicide? It's the balance of your mind which is in question, not hers, if you think that's a possibility.'

'You were pretty rough with her, sir.'

Manton looked at his sergeant in surprise. 'What are you trying to tell me?'

'Nothing, sir. If you're satisfied she'll be all right, I'm not worried. It was just that I thought she looked more than a bit forlorn.'

'As far as I'm concerned, she's still got a piece of flint for a heart and a leather hide. Don't tell me you fell for that flame-coloured hair!'

'It's just that I don't like seeing women brow-beaten, sir,' Sergeant Raikes replied loftily.

'Good grief!' Manton muttered sourly, as he got into the car and slammed the door. Not for the first time he refleced on his subordinate's unconventional approach to police problems. Or was it, perhaps, he who had been in the job so long that he had grown insensitive?

The drive back was accomplished in a brittle silence. But as Manton gazed steadily out of the passenger's window, he still remained firmly certain that Rita Bromley was no more likely to commit suicide than was the Pope suddenly to embrace the Buddhist faith.

CHAPTER TWENTY-TWO

ROGER had no idea what time Austrian police officers started work in the morning, but he left it until a quarter to ten before making his call to Kirschner. This would still give him time to catch a 'plane around mid-day if the request not to stay in Vienna was confirmed.

'Hier ist Kirschner,' announced the now familiar voice when the connection was made.

'This is Roger Elwin, Herr Kirschner . . .'

Before he could get any further, Kirschner broke in, 'You are still here? I thought you go. I sent you telephone message last night.'

'I received it,' Roger replied a trifle coolly, nettled by the other's apparent impatience for his departure, 'but I thought I'd have a final word with you before I leave.'

'Yes?'

'Is there anything further on the Fischers?'

'No.'

'You haven't yet searched the house in Grünbaumgasse?'

'One must not discuss these matters on the telephone,' Kirschner said stonily.

'I could call round and see you on my way to the airport if you like.'

'I am soon going out. You must excuse.'

Roger was left in no doubt that 'please don't stay' did fairly express Herr Kirschner's sentiments and that there was no point in trying to continue the conversation. He wondered what it was that had occasioned the change of attitude. Perhaps Herr Kirschner considered he had overstepped the bounds of protocol in pursuing his own line of enquiry at the Weinstube zum Kastanienbaum; perhaps he had learnt—though Roger couldn't for the life of him think how—of his burglarious entry of the Fischer house in Grünbaumgasse; perhaps he had rumbled him as a Scotland Yard impostor. Whatever the explanation, it remained only to bid Herr Kirschner a courteous farewell.

'I am very grateful for all your assistance,' he said, 'and I hope we shall each achieve a successful conclusion of our respective cases.'

'I hope, too,' Kirschner replied politely. 'You will send me full details of this man, yes?'

'As soon as I return.'

'Then good-bye, Herr Elwin. Have a nice journey.'

'Auf wiedersehen, Herr Kirschner.'

A few hours later, Roger was airborne. As he munched his way through a succession of tasteless items which the stewardess had handed him on a tray, he began to give thought to how he was going to play his cards on return. Tony Dayne was still his client and it was Tony Dayne whom he most wanted to see. Unfortunately, it was unlikely he'd be able to do this before he saw Manton.

He, Roger Elwin, might believe that he now had the glimmerings of an idea of the background of the whole extraordinary case, but the basic problem of his client's predicament was no nearer a solution.

CHAPTER TWENTY-THREE

'HAVE you anything to declare, sir?'

Roger looked at the poker-faced young Customs officer and shook his head impatiently. 'No, nothing.'

'Are you resident in the United Kingdom?'

'Yes.'

'Where have you just come from?'

'Vienna.'

Was it his imagination or did the Customs officer's interest perceptibly quicken? At all events, he now said, 'Open your bag if you please, sir.'

Roger assumed an expression of weary frustration. There was something about air travel, for all the cosseting, which delivered one at the other end frayed and tetchy and all too ready to pick a quarrel. The impassive civility of the Customs officers was a provocation in itself.

The officer stuck a hand beneath Roger's crumpled pyjamas which lay on top of the case and gently felt around. Then chalking his mark on the end of the case, he murmured a polite, 'Thank you, sir.'

Roger felt momentarily almost sorry for him. Theirs must be a hum-drum life, with such highlights as the discovery of a consignment of hashish in a secret compartment of someone's suitcase few and far between.

To his delight, Carol was waiting for him at the exit from the Customs Hall. She flung herself into his arms and kissed him warmly. 'I only got your cable an hour ago,' she said, 'but Mr. Arkwright was terribly nice and said I could leave early. I made it sound as if you were returning from an expedition to the Gobi Desert and I hadn't seen you for years.'

He grinned at her happily. 'Forty-eight hours in Vienna, as I've just spent, is every bit as adventurous as any old expeditions to the Gobi Desert. Wait till we're in the car and you shall have a blow-by-blow account. Meanwhile it feels like years since I saw you and I can hardly wait to kiss you again.'

'When we get to the car, there are too many people about here.'

He slipped an arm round her waist and they pushed their way toward the main exit. 'How English!'

'Well, do you like being seen necking in the middle of a fat crowd?' she asked with a giggle.

'Perhaps not in this particular crowd,' he replied, glancing about him with an expression of distaste, 'they all look so bored and unimaginative.'

'How else do you expect people to look at an airport? They're all either expecting to crash in flames or are still overcome with surprise that they didn't. Either way, their minds have congealed.'

When they were in the car, Roger made good his wish, and it was several minutes before he turned his attention to the business of driving. On the way to his cottage he gave Carol a full account of his stay in the Austrian capital. When he reached the end, she said in an awed tone, 'It sounds like something out of a Hitchcock film. I had no idea you were going to run such risks.'

'Nor did I, or I wouldn't have gone. The thing is what do I do now?'

'How much are you going to tell Superintendent Manton?'

'I've told him most of it already on the telephone.'

'What about the photograph?'

He shook his head. 'No, I've not mentioned that. And I shan't until I've had an opportunity of talking to Dayne. After all, he still has first claim on my services. I'll go and see him in Brixton to-morrow.'

'What's going to be his reaction when he learns that you went to Vienna against his wishes?'

Roger expelled a deep breath. 'I've no idea. But if he has any sense he'll accept the fait accompli and answer my questions. That's the advantage of faits accomplis over events still in prospect.'

Carol was silent for a time, then she said with a slight shiver, 'It's an appalling story. Two people murdered a thousand miles away because of some dirty dealing over forged travellers cheques in this country.'

'That sort of thing happens when the stakes are sufficiently high, as they were in this case.'

'You really believe that the man Slater went to Vienna for the sole purpose of killing Freda Fischer?'

'It looks very much like it.'

'Then it serves him right that he got such prompt deserts.' She was thoughtful for a moment. 'It's a pity you couldn't have found out more about the Fischers and exactly what goes on behind their scenes.'

'I know. We'll have to wait for Kirschner to send us a report.'

'But do you think he will? He sounded a bit huffy at the end.'

'I think he just wanted me out of the way for some reason. I'm sure he'll keep us informed, if only because he will want to know what's happening here.' He paused. 'I keep on saying "us", but I've less idea than ever where I stand in this shifting mess.'

They arrived at Roger's cottage, and while he went upstairs to unpack and have a wash, Carol began to prepare their supper.

'There doesn't seem to be very much in the larder,' she called out. 'Will scrambled eggs and mushrooms do you, followed by cheese?'

'Splendidly.'

'Cancel the cheese offer,' she shouted back a little later. 'You shouldn't have left it in the fridge, it's like a lump of sandstone.'

'We'll have fruit instead.'

'That looks a trifle off as well.'

'Well let's hope the eggs are all right or we'll have to open one of Matthew's tins of cat-meat.'

When he came downstairs, Roger had a small packet in his hand. 'A present from Vienna,' he said, handing it over with a kiss.

In the excitement of arriving home and seeing Carol again, he had quite forgotten the brooch he had bought her at the souvenir stall at the airport. Not that he proposed telling her that. It was only a few minutes before his flight was called that he remembered that he had not got her anything. He had stuffed the brooch in his pocket and had completely overlooked its presence there when confronted by the stern young Customs officer. Not that it would have been likely to have attracted any duty, it was too cheap for that, but his conscience nevertheless gave him a quiet pang when he realised he'd been guilty of a form of deceit which he particularly despised.

'It's beautiful,' Carol said happily. 'Did it come from a very posh shop?'

'Fairly,' he replied, and quickly changed the subject. 'There's no doubt I'm going to marry the best scrambler of eggs England has ever produced.'

It was at this moment that the telephone began to ring.

'You answer it,' he said coaxingly.

'It's certain to be for you. After all, it is your house.'

'All right,' he replied wearily, and went across to the instrument which lived on a table to the right of the hearth. 'Roger Elwin here.'

'So you're back!'

He recognised Manton's voice on the line. 'I got in about an hour ago.'

'Can I come round and see you?'

Roger hesitated. He was in no hurry to see Manton and particularly didn't want him barging in now. He had other plans for the evening which didn't include the intrusion of third parties.

'I'm a bit tired. Can it wait till the morning? I'll call in and see you in my way to the office.'

'You know what this place is for interruptions. I'd prefer to have a quiet chat with you this evening if possible. I won't keep you up late.'

'All right then,' Roger replied in a thoroughly ungracious tone.

'I'll be with you in about three-quarters of an hour.'

'It's Manton, he's coming round,' he said to Carol who had gone into the kitchen to make some coffee.

'Shall I go?'

'No. If he doesn't want to talk in front of you, *he* can go.'

'I'd better make some extra coffee.'

'I suppose we'll have to offer him a cup,' Roger remarked in a grudging tone.

Manton seemed in no way put out at finding Carol in the cottage when he arrived and, to Roger's annoyance, proceeded to make himself thoroughly at home. Stirring the three lumps of sugar he'd put in his coffee, he turned to her and said with a friendly smile, 'I suppose he's told you how he's been gallivanting around Vienna at the British taxpayer's expense?'

Roger frowned. So now he was going to be reminded who had footed the bill and thereby of his obligation to present a full account of his mission.

'From what he's told me,' Carol replied lightly, 'I don't think I'd use the expression "gallivanting".'

'Nevertheless, it's more than I've been able to arrange for myself in twenty-seven years' service.'

'But I thought senior police officers were always flying off to exciting places to bring back wanted men.'

'They're the lucky minority, though I agree they usually seem to go to pretty enviable places, such as the Bahamas and Acapulco. But that's because most of the defendants who skip the country make a bee-line for the world's sun-drenched fleshpots. That is, those who are worth bringing back.

'Actually I did once get a trip abroad. I was a young detective-sergeant at the time and was sent across to Ostend to bring back a man who'd stolen a couple of thousand pounds from his employers and decamped across the channel to take up permanent residence with his Belgian mistress. I spent precisely two hours on shore and was sick both ways. I may add that everyone was sick apart from my prisoner, who passed the journey drinking light ales.'

Carol laughed as Manton reached the end of his story but Roger permitted himself no more than a wintry smile. Turning in his direction, Manton now said, 'I hope Miss Chant won't be bored if we discuss a little business. I imagine she already knows a fair amount about the case.' His tone was lightly sardonic, and he'd obviously guessed that Roger had taken her fully into his confidence despite his, Manton's, original request for absolute secrecy.

'Go ahead,' Roger said woodenly.

'*You* go ahead. You're the one with news to report.'

'I haven't anything to add to what I told you in my two telephone calls.'

'The Austrian police haven't yet taken any action against the Fischers?'

'None that Kirschner was prepared to disclose.'

'I take it he'll keep in touch with us, however?'

'He said he would.'

'Good. After your call yesterday evening, I went to see Bromley's wife. She obviously had no idea what had happened to her brother and news of his death came as a complete shock.'

'Incidentally,' Roger broke in, 'Kirschner would like you to send him Slater's full particulars.'

'I've already done that, plus a photograph.' He looked across at Carol. 'It's always much easier dealing with gentlemen who are on our books. Lew Slater had a record as long as a foot ruler.' Turning back to Roger he went on, 'I suppose

129

there's no doubt that Slater did murder the girl and was then killed by one of her family?'

'I wouldn't say any.'

'I don't know to what extent it'll be introduced into our case—that'll be for the lawyers to decide—but it seems to explain most of the loose ends.'

Roger said nothing, but wondered what Manton would say if he were to produce the snapshot which rested in his wallet. That didn't explain a loose end: it created one.

'Has a date yet been fixed for the hearing?' he enquired.

'The court is going to do that when they come up on remand the day after to-morrow.'

'You're now ready to present your case?'

'We can prove the cheques are forgeries and suggest where they came from and how they were brought into the country. Above all, we can prove possession against the boys.'

'I don't see what *evidence* you have as to the country of origin and how they reached here.'

'We're now in a position to prove that the suitcase containing the cheques was brought into the country by a girl named Freda Fischer who had arrived on a flight from Vienna.'

'How?'

'It's been identified by the Customs officer who handled it.'

Roger made a face. 'He must handle hundreds of similar ones. How can he recognise this particular one?'

'He just can. He happens to be an observant young man.'

'I don't imagine any amount of observation would have helped him unless he'd first been told what you believe to have happened. A good example, if I may say so, Superintendent, of finding the evidence to fit the facts.'

Manton raised an eyebrow. 'I'm not sure that isn't a defamatory observation.'

Roger looked across at Carol. 'Know what they do! They go along to London Airport with the case, show it to all the Customs officers and say, "Look boys, we happen to know that this case was carried through Customs by an Austrian girl named Freda Fischer on such and such a date. One of you must remember it? The quicker someone says so the better." At last its identification is fathered on to some poor guy, and before he knows what's happened, he's in the witness-box giving evidence on oath.'

'Well, what's wrong with that?' Carol asked. 'It seems the only sensible way of setting about things.'

'Thank you, Miss Chant, I won't instruct my lawyer to sue your fiancé after all,' Manton said.

Roger threw back his head and let out a long-suffering groan.

In a more serious tone, Manton went on, 'Are you proposing to see your chap before the next hearing?'

'Probably.'

'You might ask him whether Freda Fischer had been over on previous occasions and if not, who had?'

'How do you know there've been previous occasions?'

'My enquiries to date show that they'd been operating the travel agent racket for over six months. They started up in Manchester last autumn. During that time they must have received at least one other consignment of forged cheques. Possibly more.' He glanced at his watch and got up. 'You'd better let me have your report as soon as possible.'

'What report?' Roger asked with a note of surprise.

'On your trip to Vienna, of course. The Auditor-General will expect to see something in return for his money.'

CHAPTER TWENTY-FOUR

DURING their twice-daily periods of exercise in prison, it had become customary for Bromley and Armley to pair off and for Dayne and Passfield to do likewise. Max Rutter walked on his own more often than not, though he did from time to time join up with one lot or the other.

It was on the afternoon of Roger's return from Vienna, when both Bromley and Armley were called off exercise because of visitors, that Rutter sidled up and fell into step beside Dayne and Passfield. Throwing Passfield an irritable look, he said, 'I want to talk to Tony alone.' When Passfield took no notice, he went on, 'Disappear, Roy, I said I wanted to talk to Tony alone.'

'I heard you first time. Proper little dictator you're becoming. Go and try your orders on someone else. The Governor, for example.'

'O.K., Roy,' Dayne broke in, 'if Max wants to speak to me alone, you'd better leave us.'

'How do I know you're not going to fix something behind my back. After all, we're in this together, so what secrets can Max have, which I shouldn't hear?'

'Tony'll tell you later,' Rutter said with tight-lipped impatience. 'Now drop overboard.'

'Go on, Roy,' Dayne added.

With a faint toss of the head and a thoroughly sulky expression, Passfield quickened his pace and drew ahead. Within a few seconds, he was round the far side, overtaking everyone as if on the final stretch of the London to Brighton walk.

'It's about Big George,' Rutter said in a conspiratorial whisper.

'What this time?'

'He's planning to escape.'

'Out of here?' Dayne asked in surprise.

Rutter shook his head. 'No, next time we go to court.'

'How do you know?'

'I overheard him and Derek talking about it on exercise this morning.'

'Armley's in it as well?'

'Two always stand a better chance of getting away than one. Anyway, Derek's a sort of favourite nephew, he wouldn't want to leave him behind.'

'How much did you actually hear?' Dayne asked with interest.

'Quite a bit. They didn't realise I was so close behind them. When they did, they were ready to be quite nasty until I was able to satisfy them that I'd not heard anything. I pretended I'd only just come up that moment to join them.' He paused and, glancing quickly about him, went on in the same hoarse whisper, 'I didn't catch all the details, but I think the plan is to make a dash for it as we're being taken out of court at the end of the next hearing. There's only the jailer with his court list saying, "Come on, step lively you lot" as he gets ready to usher in the next prisoner, and you may have noticed that one of the doors leading out of the court is only a few feet to the right of the one we go through on our way back to the cells. I

132

reckon they stand a pretty good chance.'

'They'd stand an even better one if a diversion was created,' Dayne observed thoughtfully. Then he added, 'What are you proposing to do, Max?'

'I haven't thought. That's why I wanted to talk to you, Tony. I'm not as fit as I was. I don't reckon I'd get very far if I tried to make a dash for it. Also it's obvious that Big George and Derek are going to keep this to themselves. Once they're away, they won't spare us many thoughts.'

'Too true.' Dayne's tone carried a trace of bitter malice.

'Well, what do you think, Tony?'

'I'd like more time. We're not due to go to court until the day after tomorrow.' He gave Rutter a sly smile. 'It needs a bit of thinking about. Learnt anything else from Big George?'

'He's more than ever positive it was Freda who grassed on us.'

Dayne's expression became blank, though a muscle twitched at the angle of his jaw.

'Does he know why?'

'He hasn't told me. I suppose it has to do with the head-quarters background. He's the only one who knows anything about that.' After a pause he went on, 'I liked Freda, though I would happily slit her little throat if I could lay my hands on her now.'

'Has Big George mentioned what's happened to her?'

Rutter shook his head. 'She's obviously back where she came from, probably getting ready to peddle her cheques in some other country.'

Ever since Roger had told him of Freda's death, Dayne had watched for some sign that Bromley knew as well, but he had been disappointed. It was clear that Rutter had no knowledge of the event and Passfield, too, appeared to be completely ignorant of what had happened to her. If Bromley was aware of her death, it was quite likely that he had told Armley. And perhaps he might prove the more pliable source to tap.

'What are you thinking about, Tony?'

'Eh?'

'You suddenly looked as if your thoughts were miles away.'

Dayne made a wry grimace. 'My thoughts? I was just thinking about what you've told me.'

It was true, too, except it was fortunate that none of them were mind-readers. For the thousandth time, Dayne silently cursed the casual twist of fate which had delivered him into police hands with such disastrous results.

How disastrous he alone knew.

*   *   *

While Dayne and Rutter had been discussing him, George Bromley was being visited by his wife. He could tell that something had happened as soon as he saw her. Her face was very pale and her eyes had dark smudges beneath them. She was also sitting as though she were being held in place by an electric current.

'What's up, Rita?' he asked, without preliminaries.

'That Manton was at the house last night.' Two small white teeth caught the corner of her mouth. 'He says Lew's dead. That he's been murdered in Vienna.' She looked quickly away and said in a tight voice, 'I never wanted him to go. I thought something would happen.'

Her husband ignored the implied recrimination. 'Are the police quite certain about this?'

'Yes. Manton said they'd had a report from the police out there.'

'You don't think he may have been bluffing? Trying to frighten you into saying something?'

'No.'

'You'd better tell me exactly what he did say.'

In short, terse sentences Rita proceeded to do this. When she had finished, her husband said, 'Poor old Lew! But at least he managed to kill that treacherous bitch first.'

'I wish he'd never gone.'

'Now don't create, Rita! That won't help him or us.' He glanced round quickly to make sure that the officer on duty was out of earshot. 'Now listen very carefully to me. Remember what I told you last week.' She nodded. 'Have you done what I asked about selling the house?'

'Yes.'

'Good. And nobody knows?'

'Not a soul.'

'That's O.K. Well, it's going to be the day after tomorrow:

Derek and I have decided not to leave it any longer. And in view of what you say about Lew, it's just as well. Now you know what you've got to do? As we're being taken out of court, you've to let out a scream and pretend to faint. Make as much of a scene as you can. But it must be real good. And in the confusion which follows, we'll make a dash. All clear?'

'Won't they guess that my scream and your escape are connected?' she asked anxiously.

'They can guess as much as they like and for as long as they like. The thing is that they won't have any evidence, and without evidence they can't touch you. By the end of that day, I should be across the Channel. Sit tight until you hear from me. I'll write to you as Mrs. Brown, Poste Restante, Ealing, which means you'll have to go over there to collect the letters, and provided you make sure you're not followed they'll never get on to it. I'll let you know in each letter how you can communicate with me. And then in a few weeks time when you've settled up everything here you can join me and we'll decide where to sink our roots.' He gave her an encouraging smile. 'What d'you fancy, Rita? A nice little villa in the South of France? Or somewhere on the slopes of a Swiss mountain?'

'If only things hadn't gone wrong for poor Lew, I'd feel much more confident.'

'It's tough about Lew, but he wouldn't want us tò throw a fit of nerves. I promise you, Rita, if you do everything I've told you nothing'll go wrong and nobody'll be able to touch you, whatever they suspect. And they certainly are going to suspect. You must be prepared for Manton to try and break you down.'

'It'd take more than that bastard.'

'That's my Rita! Think of the life we're going to have in a few weeks' time.' In a small-boy's tone he added, 'Do you still love me as much as ever?'

'More,' she replied.

'See you at court, the day after tomorrow then.' She nodded. 'And, Rita!'

'Mm?'

'Be sure you make it a bloody good scream!'

CHAPTER TWENTY-FIVE

ROGER awoke the next morning feeling thoroughly ill at ease. This he invariably did when there lay ahead of him a day which he had been dreading, and Manton's visit the previous evening had done nothing to dispel the mental malaise which had been building up inside him ever since he'd left Vienna.

To make matters worse, he again cut himself shaving, he over-boiled his breakfast egg and Matthew, who normally always put in an appearance as soon as Roger came downstairs, was nowhere to be seen. Moreover, no amount of calling made him materialise. With the first touch of spring in the air, he was liable to go off on an all-night hunt, in which event Roger wouldn't see him until he returned home that evening when he would most likely be fast asleep on some forbidden surface.

When he reached his office, Miss Carne was just setting out the mail in a neat pile on his desk.

'Good morning, Miss Carne,' he said briskly.

'Good morning, Mr. Elwin. I hope you enjoyed your trip.'

'It was a working one, you know. I didn't have much time for enjoyment.'

'I've done my best to keep you free of appointments to-day as I think you'll find you have a full day's paper work in front of you.'

'Then I shan't get through it. I have to go and see Dayne in Brixton.'

Miss Carne frowned. 'Isn't he due up in court to-morrow?'

'Yes, but I have to see him before then.'

'That's unfortunate,' she said in chilly disapproval. 'I had supposed you'd be at your desk all to-day. There are one or two rather urgent matters awaiting your attention.'

'I'm afraid they'll have to wait.'

'Very well, Mr. Elwin. I'll do my best to explain if there are any 'phone calls while you're out.'

Miss Carne withdrew, leaving Roger to go through his letters. But he found he was unable to give them the concentration they required and, putting them beneath a heavy glass paper-weight, he decided the sooner he saw Dayne the better.

Brixton Prison, an uninviting destination at the best of times, now seemed doubly so as he drove through the once respectable Victorian purlieus of South London and turned into the minor road which flanked one side of the jail. Being the main remand prison for London, it resembled in many ways a high-walled transit camp, and there were few hours of the day during which arrivals and departures were not being grimly recorded. Prisoners on remand could wear their own clothes and receive mail and visitors with the frequency of patients in a hospital. They also had the over-vaunted privilege of having their meals brought in from outside. It always pleased Roger to picture Pruniers or the Savoy Grill despatching a delicate lunch of smoked Scotch salmon.and coq au vin, with half a bottle of Liebfraumilch, in a strictly anonymous van into the wasteland of South London. He supposed it might have happened but it seemed more likely that those who did avail themselves of the right belonged to the sausage, egg and chip brigade, which was much closer to his own favourite diet.

It not infrequently occurred that inmates benefited from the spartan regime of prison life, and that after a week or two their cheeks had a bloom which they hadn't known in many dissipated years. This, however, was not the case with Dayne, whose complexion had become pasty with an unhealthy puffiness around the eyes which was the more apparent in someone of such compact neatness.

He came into the interview room where Roger was waiting with an enquiring smile and one faintly quizzical eyebrow raised.

'Something happened?' he asked immediately.

'Yes. I felt I must have a chat with you before court tomorrow.'

'I'm glad, because I've got something on my mind too.'

'Oh, what's that?'

'I have it on the best authority that Bromley and Armley are going to make a break for it.' His eyes had a lively glint as he waited for his solicitor's reaction.

For a few seconds Roger said nothing though his spirit groaned under the impact of this further complicating factor which had been so casually tossed at him.

'You'd better tell me about it,' he said in a studiously neutral tone.

Dayne now did so, finishing up by saying easily, 'This can

137

be my chance to get out. I've been thinking about it, and if the police don't cock it up again, I can get away while Bromley and Armley are put back in the bag.'

'You mean that you want me to inform the police?'

Dayne looked at him pityingly. 'Well, it's a natural, isn't it? I can get clear away and it'll look as if I merely took advantage of a situation created by others.'

'Won't they immediately suspect you in those circumstances?'

'Why should they? Rutter's not going to tell them that he grassed to me and you're not going to tell them that I grassed to you. This is their plan all the way.' He gave Roger a sly grin. 'Unhappily, it doesn't work out for them, but by chance it does me a bit of good.'

Roger was silent again. Heaven knows, this certainly did seem to offer a solution to what was daily becoming a more intolerable problem. It would suit the police, by ridding them of an awkward prisoner whom they'd not wanted to arrest in the first place. It would suit him, Roger, for the same reason. And it would do more than satisfy the object of all their embarrassment.

'Very well,' he said at last, 'I'll pass this on to Superintendent Manton.'

'And for God's sake tell him to fix things properly this time. If anything goes wrong again, I'll see that the whole country knows what a bleeding lot of thick-heads they are. Incidentally, they'll have to go through all the motions of looking for me, otherwise Big George's suspicions will be aroused.' As an afterthought, he added, 'He's not stupid all the time.' Roger nodded, while Dayne launched into details of his plan for escape.

When he had finished, Roger asked with a note of interest, 'What were you going to do if I'd not come to see you today?'

'I'd have got a message to you somehow, but it's certainly made easier your turning up like this. Now, it's your turn to tell me what's on your mind.'

The rather smug expression on his face vanished abruptly as Roger said, 'I've just come back from Vienna. Despite your wishes, I felt it was my duty to go and have a nose-around there.' He had no intention of telling Dayne that the police had financed his trip and had been appraised of its results. That is, of everything save one small item. 'Though a solicitor has to act on his client's instructions,' he went on, 'that doesn't mean he can't use his own initiative if he feels it may be in his client's ultimate interest that he should do so.' Roger was by no means convinced of this perhaps doubtful premise, but he felt it necessary to justify his action professionally to Dayne, who was beginning to show signs of impatience.

'All right, Mr. Elwin, so you went to Vienna when I asked you not to. What's done is done, so cut the explanations and get on to the facts.'

'I had a look round the Fischer's house,' Roger said doggedly, and awaited Dayne's reaction.

'You have the advantage over me there. I've never even been to Vienna.' Dayne's tone was sarcastic.

'I met some of Freda's relations.'

'You still have the advantage over me.'

'Isn't it time you told me the truth?'

Dayne looked at him in amazement. 'I thought you'd come here to tell me something important. I've got nothing further to tell you, Mr. Elwin.'

Without a further word, Roger pulled the snapshot out of his pocket and pushed it across the table toward Dayne.

'A very good likeness,' he remarked drily.

'Where'd you get hold of this?'

'It was tucked into a photograph frame on the bedside table in Freda Fischer's bedroom, if you want all the details.'

It was a full minute before Dayne looked up. Then he said, 'Well, what do you want to know?'

'How it got there?'

'That's easy. I gave it to her.'

'Up until now you've always told me that you'd not met the girl before the night you were arrested.'

Dayne shrugged. 'Naturally.'

'I gather it's not true?'

'No, Mr. Elwin, it's not true,' he replied with mock contrition.

Roger was thoughtful for a few seconds, then with sudden decision he said, 'I think we might be able to strike a bargain.'

'Let's hear it.'

'You want me to arrange matters with the police so that you

can make your escape to-morrow, I want you to tell me the truth.'

'About what?'

'Everything.'

'And if I don't?'

'You might find yourself back here in Brixton prison to-morrow evening.'

Dayne looked at him with an expression of anger which turned to one of wry acceptance as Roger stared stonily back at him.

'I didn't think you were that sort of lawyer,' he said nastily.

'If you mean what I think you mean, I'm not that sort. On the other hand, I don't see why, after all the headaches this case has given me, I shouldn't have the satisfaction of knowing what really took place. It's as simple as that.'

'That's all very well, but who else is going to know?'

'No one.'

'You won't inform the police of anything I tell you?'

Roger thought hard for a second. In the first place, Dayne was his client and communications which passed between solicitor and client were privileged and confidential. His main concern was that he might be made a party to some highly embarrassing disclosure which would increase the strain on his sense of moral duty. But this seemed unlikely in the circumstances, and he decided that he was prepared to risk it. The overriding factor was that the police had the miscreants under lock and key and had sufficient evidence already to secure their conviction, so that anything Dayne might now tell him would merely be filling in the gaps of his own knowledge. Indeed, probably no more than confirming what he already surmised.

'I give you my assurance that I shan't tell the police anything.'

Dayne made a sucking noise with his lips and said, 'Well, then, here goes. Freda Fischer and I were going to get married. She'd been over a few times before with the cheques and we clicked from the very first. But, of course, none of the others knew this. What used to happen was that she'd bring the stuff over and then stay a few days and I'd see her then on the quiet. The whole business of selling the cheques was controlled from Vienna. When they decided to establish an organisation here for dealing with them, George Bromley was approached—

Heaven knows how anyone ever came to recommend him for running the sort of outfit required—and he recruited the rest of us. Vienna was very insistent that everything be handled behind the respectable front of a travel agency, but, of course, Big George soon tired of all the trouble that involved and he began cashing cheques himself and being generally big-headed. He tried telling Vienna that he knew their business better than they did and naturally they weren't going to put up with that. I was then secretly asked to take over the set-up in this country—that was Freda's suggestion, of course. And once that was fixed, all we had to do was disband the old organisation.'

'For which you enlisted the help of the police,' Roger remarked acidly.

'Precisely. It should have been a perfect plan. In exchange for my information, they were prepared to let me escape and then, in a few weeks time, business could have started up again under fresh cover and with me in charge. It was the perfect plan in theory but it turned out lousily.' He glanced at Roger from lowered eyes. 'Though it wasn't really the police's fault that I was arrested.'

'Well, go on.'

'You see, Freda should have been well clear of the bungalow before the police ever arrived, but Big George was determined to have a showdown with her that evening, so she didn't get away and the raid took place while she was still there. In the circumstances, there was only one thing to do. I had to make quite sure that she escaped and in achieving that I got myself arrested. You see, I passed her through the gap which it was arranged I should use, which meant I had to take my chance elsewhere.'

'Why? Why couldn't you have escaped with her?'

'Well, that really would have pointed the finger. As it is, Big George came to the conclusion that it was she who grassed, and you know what's happened to her.'

'Wouldn't he have come to the same conclusion about you if the plan had gone as it was meant to?'

'No, because he had no reason to connect me with Freda or Vienna. He'd almost certainly still have suspected her.' The corners of his mouth turned suddenly down. 'Where I underestimated Big George was in assuming that he wouldn't dare attack on the enemy's home-ground.'

'What was, or should I say is, the Vienna set-up?'

An artful smile crossed Dayne's features. 'I think I've told you all that our bargain requires.'

'Maybe,' Roger said amenably. This was something which he felt sure he'd learn later from Manton. Otherwise his knowledge was now complete. He rose. 'I think I can say that this has been the most fruitful visit I've ever paid a Brixton client. Till to-morrow.'

'Till to-morrow,' Dayne repeated. Then in an anxious tone he went on, 'You're sure you know exactly what to say to Manton?'

'Leave it to me.'

'I can't help feeling that Bromley will have arranged for some sort of distraction to take place, which'll make the whole thing more natural-looking.'

'I should think that's quite likely.'

Dayne observed him in silence for a while, then, shaking his head, he said doubtfully, 'I hope you don't mind my saying so, Mr. Elwin, but you're a bit of a surprise. In a curious sort of way, I find I trust you, despite your recent threat to blackmail me. I must hope it isn't trust misplaced.'

'Yes, that's all you can do, isn't it?' Roger replied in an unfriendly voice.

The truth was, as he recognised on his journey home, that he entertained distinctly ambivalent feelings toward his unusual client. He admired the resilience and generally infectious good humour. He was even able to admire the shrewdness and the opportunism. But he did find himself put out by the amorality and the lack of any genuine warmth. He had never met Freda Fischer and it might have been that marriage would have produced an unsuspected vein of humanity in her husband, but Roger could only conclude from Dayne's reaction to his fiancée's death that it was buried deep, if it existed at all. Maybe he felt it more than he showed, but it seemed that he regarded it as nothing more than an untoward and regrettable incident.

Roger sighed. He would long remember to-day. However, he hoped that his forthcoming interview with Manton would turn out to be as trouble-free as the one which lay behind him.

CHAPTER TWENTY-SIX

MANTON listened to him in silence with hands folded beneath his chin. Once or twice he made gentle hissing sounds through his teeth while his gaze strayed round the room, but his concentration never wavered.

When Roger finished, he said, 'He's a nasty little piece, isn't he?'

'Can an informant be anything else? You don't judge them by the normal code-book, surely?'

'True.'

'And, anyway, you ought to be grateful to him. As a result of this, you'll frustrate Bromley's escape and be shot of Dayne.' With feeling he added, 'And heaven knows you ought to welcome that eventuality.'

'And you, too!'

'Certainly. But remember I was only got into this mess thanks to you.'

Manton continued to look thoughtful. After a pause he said, 'It's all right, I'm won over. I'm merely trying to think of all the possible snags and repercussions.'

'The biggest snag and the loudest repercussion will be if one of your chaps rugger tackles Dayne as he's making his getaway,' Roger remarked tartly.

'We'll see that doesn't happen. I think the best thing will be for us to lock the door which, according to Dayne, they're proposing to dash through and he can be told to make his escape through the door on the bench. That leads into the magistrates' corridor, which will be deserted, and at the end of that lies an exit which brings him into the magistrates' car park. That should also be deserted. In fact he should be well away before anyone who doesn't know what's going on can collect their wits.'

'Will you have extra officers in court?'

'One or two perhaps, but I shan't warn anyone who doesn't already know Dayne's position. For example, it'll look much better if the jailer who wheels the prisoners in and out is genuinely taken by surprise.'

'Won't you have to provide an explanation for securing a door which is normally left unlocked?'

'Leave that to me.' Abruptly, he asked, 'Did Dayne give you any other interesting bits of information?'

'Nothing.'

'He didn't say what his plans were for afterwards?'

Roger shook his head. 'I don't think he's got beyond contemplating his complete disappearance.'

'I bet you he has.'

'Well, he didn't tell me.'

'You haven't said how he reacted to news of your visit to Vienna?'

'Calmly.'

'Didn't he say anything at all?'

'Why should he have? After all, Bromley was the only one who had dealings with headquarters.'

'I suppose he's never told you why he grassed on them.'

'No, but you have. You told me it was because he was fed up with the way things were being run and because he thought Bromley and the others had it in for him.'

Manton sighed. 'That's certainly what he told us. I just wondered if you'd learnt anything different.'

Roger shook his head as though the matter held no great interest for him. When he returned to his office it was to find Miss Carne at her most huffy.

'I'd expected you back long before now,' she said reprovingly. 'I 'phoned the prison two hours ago and they said you'd left.'

'I had another call to make on my return journey.'

'You'll find a number of messages on your desk,' she went on, dismissing his explanation as undeserving of comment, 'so perhaps you'll let me know in which order you'd like me to get the calls.'

He nodded and passed into his office. The first thing he did do was to write a brief memo to the office manager enquiring when Miss Carne was due to retire. He grinned happily as he suddenly pictured her tendering her resignation with effect from the Ides of March. Perhaps he could even engineer it.

CHAPTER TWENTY-SEVEN

ROGER approached court the next day with all the enthusiasm of one plunging on to a battlefield. To say that he felt nervous and apprehensive would be understating his emotions.

The first person he met on arrival was Bromley's solicitor, Mr. Woodside, who came up to him with an air of importance and said, 'We're making an all-out attack on the prosecution for the scandalous delay in presenting their case. I gather the court is proposing to fix a date in the week after next, but we're going to urge an immediate start. I imagine you'll go along with us on this.'

Roger nodded. Then remembering his part, he said, 'I agree we should press for an earlier hearing than the week after next. It's extremely unfair keeping our clients locked up all this time without knowledge of the case against them.'

'Of course it's the old, old story,' Mr. Woodside broke in briskly. 'Acting on information, the police burst in and make arrests and then afterwards set about looking for evidence to support the charge they've brought. Quite scandalous.' He lowered his voice. 'Have you discovered anything to indicate who the informant was?'

'I gathered it was some girl who afterwards escaped to Austria.'

'That's your information, too? Interesting! My chap hasn't said a word to me, but putting two and two together, I had reached the same conclusion. I think we've got a run with our defence, though there are one or two awkward hurdles to be surmounted.' He glanced toward the main door. 'Excuse me, I see Mrs. Bromley.'

He left Roger's side and hurried over to Rita, who had just arrived and was peering about her with a strained and anxious expression.

Roger entered the jailer's office.

' 'Morning, Mr. Elwin,' the jailer said. 'The van's just arrived. Want to see your chap?'

'Please.'

'Everything O.K.?' Dayne asked in an eager whisper when Roger was shown into his cell.

'Listen carefully, while I give you your instructions.'

'I'm listening.'

When Roger had finished, Dayne merely nodded, but his eyes were shining and he kept on wiping the palms of his hands down the sides of his trousers. As Roger was being let out of the cell, Dayne said in a voice loud enough for his neighbours to hear, 'You will have another bash at getting me bail, won't you, Mr. Elwin?'

Roger took his place in court and tried to assume the expression of dogged boredom which was his normal appearance while waiting for a case to be called. Mr. Woodside came and sat beside him muttering darkly about counsel having been held up by the traffic. On his right sat a representative from the Director of Public Prosecutions office who had come to show goodwill and to refute the more outrageous observations which appeared likely to fall from his brethren on the other side.

Glancing about him, Roger noticed Rita Bromley sitting alone in the back row of the public gallery. It did occur to him that she had selected the least accessible seat in the whole court-room, though the significance of this didn't dawn on him at the time. Of Manton, there was no sign at all.

It seemed an age before the swing-door from the jailer's office opened and Bromley, Rutter, Armley, Passfield and Dayne followed each other through and into the wooden pen which passed for a dock. Their expressions revealed nothing, and if three of them were experiencing any of Roger's tautness of nerves it certainly couldn't be detected. It was as though from a great distance that he heard the Director's representative ask for a further remand and inform the Court that the prosecution would be ready to proceed on the day which he understood was suitable to everyone for the full hearing.

When he sat down, Bromley's counsel, who had arrived in the end, stood up and made an acid contribution. Solicitors for the other defendants injected a little further poison into the atmosphere and then the chairman of the bench was looking at Roger.

'I associate myself with everything that has been said by my learned friends and have nothing further to add,' he said with a painfully dry throat.

He was on the verge of sitting down again when Dayne's voice cut in behind him.

'Bail! Ask for bail!'

With a muttered apology, both to the bench and to his client, he made the further plea, feeling, as he did so, more and more as if he were in a nightmare realm of distorted reality.

The two magistrates conferred briefly together and then announced that there would be a remand to the date fixed and that bail in each case was refused.

'This way,' the jailer called out mechanically as he turned toward the swing door.

Passfield was actually through it, with Rutter just behind him when a paralysing scream, which turned swiftly into a ghastly moan, shattered the atmosphere. There was a thud, where Rita had been sitting, and at the same time a sound of feverish scuffling broke out just behind Roger's back. All he could do, however, was to stare rigidly ahead of him. He heard Manton's voice call out, 'Guard all the doors.' Then: 'Sit on his head.'

The sounds of skirmish continued for a minute or two, and then with the final distant clanging of a cell door, all became silent again. Manton came back into court and said in a grim voice, 'One prisoner managed to get away.'

The magistrates shook themselves like survivors of an air-raid and pointed to the door which led from the bench.

'Someone dashed through there,' said the chairman with difficulty.

Manton immediately disappeared again and could be heard shouting orders somewhere outside.

Addressing the row of lawyers, the clerk said, 'More would have got away if that door hadn't been locked. That was the way two of them tried to go. It's normally always open, but someone smashed the window in the corridor immediately outside during the night and I knew from past experience that if it wasn't locked, it would rattle with the draught until we were all driven mad. Perhaps in the circumstances we ought to be grateful to whoever it was who did it.' With a faint smile he added, 'Probably one of our past customers getting his own back.' He glanced to the back of the court. 'Does anyone know what happened there?'

'A woman fainted, sir,' announced a portly constable. 'She's being attended to outside.'

He turned to the magistrates. 'Perhaps you might think it sensible to adjourn for five minutes, sir? That'll give us all time for our nerves to settle again.'

As Roger left the court, feeling wrung out and weak at the knee joints, he could only reflect that it was the oddest circumstance in which to see the last of a client.

CHAPTER TWENTY-EIGHT

THREE days later, as Roger was wrestling with a particularly tricky conveyance for a client whose esteem he had originally won when defending him on a charge of drunken driving, Miss Carne's voice came on the line to announce that Superintendent Manton wished to speak to him.

'He says it's important,' she remarked in a tone which clearly indicated her own disbelief of this. 'I told him you were busy . . .'

'No, all right, put him through.'

'Good morning,' Manton said cheerfully a second later. 'I thought you'd be interested to hear that your friend Kirschner has not been wasting his time. They've arrested Ernst Fischer —that's Freda's brother, the one you met at the café—for the murder of Lew Slater. He admits killing him but is, I gather, likely to get off fairly lightly since he was avenging his sister's death.'

'I thought that sort of thing only operated in Latin countries.'

'Don't ask me and I may have got it wrong anyway. The thing is we now have confirmation that it was Slater who killed Freda.'

'And what about the forgery aspect?'

'I was just coming on to that. You were right to have your suspicions about the basement at old man Fischer's house. They found a complete forger's outfit down there, including a whole lot of new and expensive equipment. Forgery appears to have been the old chap's pastime, while his son and daughter and a couple of nephews handled the commercial side. Quite a little family business they ran, with outlets for their products in Italy, France and Tangier, as well as here. Kirschner reckons their profits can be counted in tens of thousands. Apparently, they were proposing to make half a million and then melt away to splash around in South America for the rest of their days.'

'Did he mention how it all started?'

'Casually, like so many successful schemes. The old man is an expert engraver and used to work for a bank, and when ill-health forced his early retirement he carried on his engraving as a hobby and then, I gather, one of his family saw the commercial possibilities. And so it started.'

'Has he been arrested, too?'

'I'm not quite clear from Kirschner's report, but I imagine the Austrian police will be taking proceedings against him and the others.'

'Well, thanks for letting me know.'

'There is one more thing.'

'What's that?'

'Kirschner seems to have been a trifle upset at your misleading him into believing you were from Scotland Yard.'

Roger let out a snort. 'He misled himself, you mean. I never said a single word to suggest that.'

Manton chuckled. 'We must be more careful next time we send you on an assignment.'

'Don't worry, there won't be a next time. From now on, I'm going to be firmly on one side or the other. No more walking the legal tightrope for me.'

'You have to do it every time you defend a guilty man,' Manton observed sunnily. 'That's what I admire about your lawyer's consciences, they have built-in units of self-justification.'

'I refuse to be provoked by such an outrageous statement. And coming from a police officer, too!'

After a further by-line of mild banter, Roger rang off and summoned Miss Carne for dictation. This was something which always required the greatest mustering of his mental determination. It was like a stranger asking Queen Victoria to play noughts and crosses.

When he arrived home that evening, Carol was reading the evening paper. He mixed a drink and flopped down beside her. Looking up, she said, 'There's a bit about Dayne in the paper.'

'He hasn't been caught?' Roger asked in an anxious voice.

'No, not that. It was to the effect that the police now thought he was out of the country.'

'Thank heaven for that. I wonder if he is.'

'Why else should the police say so?'

'Manton may have noised it abroad in order to take some of the steam out of the search for him.'

Carol studied him thoughtfully for a second or two. Then stepping across, she kissed him lightly on the mouth.

'You really are very glad to be out of that case, aren't you, sweet?'

'Tremendously. I can now follow the trial of the others with real bystander's interest. As, I imagine, will Tony Dayne, wherever he may be.'

THE END

www.ingramcontent.com/pod-product-compliance
Ingram Content Group UK Ltd.
Pitfield, Milton Keynes, MK11 3LW, UK
UKHW040436280225
455666UK00003B/118